A raindrop has seen the rise and fall of civilizations and survived deserts of ice and sand. However, despite all of her adventures, she has lost the magic of being alive. That is, until a gust of wind—or perhaps a twist of fate—sends her face-to-face with a lowly rock. But what good could possibly come from a conversation with a rock? Turns out, this is no ordinary rock. This particular rock watches the world around him evolve in the most astonishing of ways, and he can almost touch the hand wielding such bewildering and obvious might. From their sudden encounter, two things spark between them: a friendship and a spiritual quest.

(continued on back cover)

The Rock And The Raindrop

A Space in Time

Bjorn Wythette

The Rock and the Raindrop — A Space in Time
Copyright © 2019 Bjorn Wythette
All rights reserved
Print Edition ISBN: 978-0-578-51272-3
Published by Trusty Dusty Enterprises

For inquiries regarding this book, please email:
rockinraindrop7@aol.com

This is a work of fiction, any resemblance to a rock or raindrop
in or near any given location is purely coincidental. However,
just between you and me bedraggled but cheerful self, all of
the characters found herein were faithfully recorded. Their
conversations are presented in full and intact.

For any someone, or someone's, who may so deign to pirate
this timeless work of art, in whole or in part, find a chair, take
a breath, then have a cookie and try working that one through.

Front cover in part by Amie McCracken. Some elements of image
furnished by NASA. Back cover: location of aurora borealis: Naryan-
Mar, Nenets Autonomous Area, Russia.

Special thanks to Erin Typo Willard: editor extraordinaire.
Back cover and interior designed by Tamian Wood, Beyond Design
International at www.BeyondDesignInternational.com

There are things known, and there are things unknown.
In between are the doors.
Jim Morrison

Prelude

She was an altogether beautiful raindrop. Her outer edges glistened as she passed through intermittent rays of sunlight, every part of her consumed by delight as she fell effortlessly. Laughing and swirling with the other raindrops, she reveled in her joy, allowing no unwanted thought to intrude, and with each passing moment the illusion that this would last forever became more real.

Behind her lay the impenetrable windings of existence, the shifting sands of reason, and the unrelenting certainty of uncertainty. Immersing herself in the release and in the joy of celebration surrounding her, she embraced her friends and they her, and for what seemed a very long time, the world was perfect.

In the midst of her revelry, a flicker of caution nudged her ever so gently, whispering something about preparing for a landing. Coming to full shimmer, she pushed the thought away. This was all too powerful—the freedom, the exhilaration, the complete dedication to a singular purpose—this was what every raindrop lived for, and every part of her was glad.

Time will have its way, though, and the voice returned. Yielding to the reality, she began to focus. There wasn't much past the tree line except a barren stretch of rock, and if the wind held its course she would surely land there. An unpleasant prospect, there was little doubt.

The wind . . . how fickle the wind.

This thought scampered through her agile mind as she weighed what chance the wind might find favor toward her. And as lightning danced in the distance, her thoughts shifted, wavering momentarily, and in that moment a vision formed. She wasn't sure what to make of it, then all too quickly she understood—forces were aligning in an odd way. Seemed there would be a reckoning; for whom she wasn't sure, nor was it clear the nature thereof, but the premonition was strong, and there would be no escape. Even so, her shimmer brightened once more as she flowed within the currents, for as close as that time may be, it was not just yet.

He was an altogether unassuming rock. Nothing in his outward appearance would suggest he was anything other than ordinary. No one went out of their way to include him in conversation, and seldom did anyone ask his opinion. This would rumple the world of most any other rock, as they are by and large a gregarious lot, but he preferred his estrangement, to the point that most thought him slow or at least odd. And though disparaging remarks were rare, when tossed his direction he'd field them with bonhomie and shrug in his amiable way, 'cause truth be told, he wasn't all that sure about them either.

That he was different was a mystery to him, for they were all cast from the same material, and they all had, in varying degrees, a plane of gem that ran through them. What set him apart, he sometimes thought, was his penchant for taking mental journeys. There were times, when on his excursions, he would cross the plane and it would stir him deeply. His vision would sharpen and take on new perspectives as he watched the world move in astonishing and incomprehensible ways. He could perceive traces of an intelligence working quietly behind the scenes, moving in a curious combination of coordination and happenstance. At times it even made him wonder if there wasn't more to being a rock than it might seem, for he desired above all things to discover the nature of this unfolding design, this cleverly hidden portrait of undeniable motive.

Having worked through the early morning hours on a series of computations, none of them really going anywhere, he put his thoughts aside and fell into an easy, wholesome reminiscence. Rummaging through the years, he came upon a time when there were no trees at all, when life was raw and desolate, when nothing moved save earth and wind. And he remembered how things had slowly begun to change, and how over time change brought with it the grasses of the field.

A new age of promise had unfolded before them, one filled with spontaneity and grace of movement. But, even with that, no one in their wildest dreams dared imagine the fields were only precursors to the magnificent collection of trees that would one day march in and call this home. With the intertwining of grass and tree, a richly woven splendor settled upon what was once a barren landscape. The world was so much more interesting now, and he thought about that. What purpose lay beyond his reach? And where was it all going? He just couldn't understand why he couldn't understand.

Before dozing off, he decided to review the day's work: "Let's see here: one plus two is three; two and three becomes five; three and five is still eight; five and eight is thirteen; eight and thirteen is . . . three sevens. A lot of prime numbers in there . . . and the progression . . . what is it about the progression? Got to find a different perspective."

Searching for a key that would open the door to anything resembling a new perspective, his eyes moved toward the river. Oh, how he loved to watch the river. He loved the way it bent, the way it moved within its own rules, pressing ever against some unknown force, finding joy without contemplation. Where did it come from and where did it go? Always in the same place yet always moving, as if carrying with it some immutable secret, a secret shared perhaps only with the wind.

He often imagined the river in some way held kinship with the wind, for they alone reveled in their hurry and were matchless in their charm. And though, much to his puzzlement, the wind wasn't always there, when it was he could feel its mysterious force move in patterns primal and familiar—willful patterns impossible to read, patterns one moment adorned with whimsy, the next filled with purpose and intent.

Shifting toward the horizon, he focused on that enigmatic line that split his world in two. One side held complexities beyond count, the other carried the sun, moon, and stars. And while they seemed simple enough . . . he had his doubts. "So many things come and go in so many ways," he said quietly. "Well, there's plenty of time to think it all through." Resting within the assurance that answers would one day unfold, he closed his eyes and drifted toward that long, slow, transcendental sleep only a rock can sleep.

Part One

There are forces in the universe that show themselves with delight, and there are those that prefer anonymity, working quietly with determination and purpose, providing support; unifying, coordinating, and watching. Life is spread among the stars, and energies flow, energies interwoven within matter, mind and spirit, energies whose purposes vary in boundless ways.

How this came to be is a mystery. That we are here and that we abound is also a mystery. That we know we abound, though, is a mystery within a mystery, an interesting and delicate balance caught within a curious swirl: energy becomes and transforms knowledge, knowledge discovers and unravels mystery, and mystery kindles curiosity.

And curiosity abounds.

Mystery and curiosity. What would one be without the other, and what part do they play within the world of spirit—a world that defies all logic, escapes all measurement, eludes definition, and moves in patterns too difficult to discern? What we *can* discern, however, emanates from those very patterns.

Throughout the universe, an array of forces move in patterns tantalizing to the eye and to the sense of profundity. The material domain moves skillfully within form, and the forces of mind draw ever steadfastly toward balance, while the forces of spirit tend toward harmony within diversity. These forces intertwine in an embrace that forges constancy amid the backdrop of an ever-changing universe, coming together with resolve and direction, seldom working in a whimsical way.

There are times, though, and they happen more often than one might think, when a bit of whimsy escapes the wind, turns its head, and finds its course.

So it is our story begins.

Chapter One

Time was up. Straining to see through the mist, the raindrop's joy melted into a quiet panic as the ground raced up to greet her. Carpeted in luxuriant velveteen splendor, what lay before her almost seemed inviting, but she was not fooled. At this pace the wind would take her past the forest and toss her headlong onto that barren, godforsaken stretch of rock. There was a chance the wind would ease and she could catch the last cradle of leaves, but chances didn't seem in her favor.

In the eternity of the moment, she held her breath. With the last fading embers of hope nearly gone, there was a turning of direction and the slightest notion of release. When the wind eased altogether the raindrop smiled, took one last swirl, and fell gracefully toward a soft comfortable landing.

Then came the gust.

As the uppermost leaves slid by in helpless unreal slow motion, she closed her eyes, offered a silent prayer, and hit the rock hard.

Consciousness—window to the wonders of the universe—a gift we take for granted, but when all is said and done it is, in reality, a mystery—unfathomable, marvelous, and rather clever when one thinks about it.

Of this the raindrop was unaware, was unaware of anything until a single pale light came into view from some indeterminable place. Wondering what it could possibly be, there came upon her a familiar strength, and once the slender tendrils of resolve fastened one to the other, she reached deep into her reserves and began to collect herself.

Things didn't go well at first, but her struggle prevailed, and once fully collected, she focused. What came into view was a harsh and alien world. In shocked disbelief, she surveyed the rock's broad expanse and managed a sentence:

"Got to be a way off this thing."

With a steely silence she took in the details. There wasn't much here; most of the contours led to traps, and the one line that seemed promising proved to end nowhere, except for that minor twist that . . . what was *that*? She moved down a ridge and banked off a crest to get a closer look. What had been obscured by the forest and by the angle of her descent was a small but brisk stream winding directly under the rock's northern edge. If she could manage, she thought, she might be able to work her way toward, and fall directly into, the one place she called home. This thought filled her with anticipation and her pace quickened, for a rock's tightly knit realm of dour stillness was no place for a lady.

As the raindrop's thoughts bent toward the river, the rock watched, from his semi-slumber, the world slowly change around him. A cool, deliberate flow ran through his fissures, a flow filled with bits of debris that searched patiently for signs of weakness, slowly changing his shape as they smoothed his edges and deepened miniature ravines.

He watched sand swell in a timeless dance as it shifted obediently, found places to rest, then shifted once more, moving contentedly to the rhythmic patter of a soft and welcome rain. He watched and marveled. What hand moved in such a way, wielding its might over the realm, joining seamlessly disparate elements of nature, binding them one to the other according to some infinitely complicated plan? He wondered how such a thing had come to be, how it all worked, and why the other rocks couldn't find it within themselves to see the magic that surrounded them.

Sometimes the derision that accompanied their lack of interest in his endeavors left him baffled, even a little sad. Nevertheless, his chosen path comforted him in bountiful ways: his ever-expanding capacity to see things hidden from his indolent and jaded brethren only emboldened his sense of adventure and spurred his desire to understand the way time brought to light the unfolding mysteries of existence. He knew there were underlying forces that showed themselves only to those who wanted to see, and he would lie in wait, wondering what delicate inspiration might next come to pass.

While the rock nestled around his thoughts, the raindrop moved with resolve, carefully winding her way into place, hoping there would be no unforeseen circumstance barring her escape. This was always the tricky part, and she had no illusions.

But time was of the essence, and *there be a river*.

Somewhere in that moment, however, her eyes began to soften, taking in the horizon with a wisp of longing. And as they did so there came upon her a breath of wind, and the wind carried with it a hint of trepidation, and as with the premonition, she knew not what to make of it.

Though it did give her pause.

However brief.

Brushing the feeling aside, she removed her gaze and by chance caught a glimpse of the rock's eyes as they began to close. There was an expression about them she'd never seen: a faint curiosity mixed with a touch of loneliness, an impression that moved her, much to her surprise, to offer an apology for disturbing his slumber.

The rock yawned and made a rumble of dismissal, hoping that would be that, for as much as he loved the beauty of movement and the range of symphony raindrops achieved as a group, there had never been profit in talking to any of them.

"Well, who wants to talk to you anyway?" she said under her breath. "Why is it always so awkward? Landings are so imprecise, you'd think . . . "

As the raindrop fumbled from one side of reason to the other, the rock crept from his somnolence, finding cause to enjoy the moment. He had never seen a raindrop carry on so. But he detected a sense of hidden delight in her manner, and seeing her in this way, there came over him an unexpected playfulness. Unable to resist, he broke into her complaint:

"Because otherwise life would be perfect, and no one's ready for that, not even Your Highness."

He fully expected her to fluster, make some feeble attempt at reconciliation, fill the air with nonsense and be on her way. This raindrop, however, turned around, stared at him for a moment, then narrowed her eyes.

"Is that so? You want to . . . wait a second . . . What?"

Confused by her response, he couldn't help but think of the countless times these mysterious creatures would scurry and scuttle here and about then be gone. Never had any of them spoken to him in more than a trifling, and never had he been able to bridge the gap, draw them into meaningful conversation. It just couldn't be done.

His eyes opened a little wider, for now a raindrop of a different character moved before him, one with a sparkle in her eye and a fire in her belly, one who carried herself with dignity, carried herself with elegance and grace. And he thought:

Ooh my. What to do . . . what to do.

Unfamiliar with raindrop etiquette, he tossed clarity around for a bit, then thought about obfuscation, eventually landing somewhere in the middle.

"I simply meant you make a great deal out of not a whole lot."

He wasn't sure how far that would go to assuage an unintended offense, but from her immediate reaction, one of befuddled consternation, it seemed to have been enough. And once again he fell into a quiet ease as he listened to the rustle of leaves, the patter of rain, and the distant rhythms of the river. The satiny soft whispers of sleep were slowly closing in, when there came upon him a stirring, its source distant and obscure.

As the raindrop occupied herself with the details of her imminent departure, the rock's eyes rolled wide. Studying the dynamics of what had been a fairly strong pulse, it occurred to him there may be more to this moment than it would seem. Watching the raindrop move within her elegance, an epiphany wandered onto the landscape of his contemplation. At first it was but a glimmer buried somewhere in the shadows of his depths, then with a swiftness rare in a rock's world, he began to entertain a notion, to actually think that this beautiful but curious itinerant perhaps, in some way, held the key to mysteries that lay beyond his grasp.

The raindrop, however, was buried deep in her own thoughts.

She was hanging on his one ragged edge, muttering, "Your Highness . . . can you believe . . . where does he get off . . . never wanted . . . goofy rock anyway," and watching the river flow, when she found herself unable to resist the temptation to turn back one last time, for never had she seen a rock's eyes fully open.

The rock took note and began a slow hum, and though she understood not a word, she moved back a little, for the melody carried a strange and simple beauty:

"What subtle breeze blows through yonder gate, 'tis the lord of hesitation, 'tis the captain of her fate," were the lyrics that ran through the rock's fissures. And he well knew if that fate were to bend his direction, he would have to find his bearing quickly, even though this would be the second time in as many minutes.

Not a rock's forte.

But this was an inspired moment.

"I know you think we're slow, and I would have no quarrel with that . . . it's just that, in a world where differences abound, you, my friend, are an enigma. There are times your apparent lack of discipline is baffling, as is your tendency toward movement without any discernible rationale. But sometimes, on the odd occasion, I can't help wondering if the whole isn't greater than the sum of its parts. I mean, your work can be quite remarkable. I am curious. When you are out there," his eyes swept the horizon, "what do you see?"

The moment caught her by surprise. There had been a spar and a query, neither of which she was prepared to address. It was true that rocks were considered less than stellar in almost every category, but until this moment she was unaware that they themselves suspected raindrops thought of rocks in this way. It was certainly true that any raindrop found fraternizing with a rock was looked upon with great suspicion, even disdain, and appearances must be kept at all cost as raindrops are a highly social order, without question above the station of the bereft . . . and scruffy.

Even so, a brow furrowed as she refastened her grip.

Her surprise began to deepen as she took in the depth and breadth of this dreary scrap of gray desolation. Never in her long career had she considered that a rock might be interested in anything other than whatever it is rocks do. She had always been left with the impression they were no more than gruff, crude creatures of dubious habit.

She watched from some distant part of her mind as the world she knew began to turn upside down. Cracks began forming, tearing at the foundation of long-held beliefs; fissures opened, swallowing completely the notion of invincibility and sovereignty. Most crushing of all was the realization that she never really paid attention to what she saw, nor had any meaningful thought been given to the reason for her existence. The immense depth of this realization triggered a series of events deep within. She wound through corridors, each one emptying into some new and astonishing pathway, taking her further from the world she knew. Soon she found herself standing before a door. As it opened, her considerable lifetime flashed before her and a picture so overwhelmingly profound came into view that all she had ever known fell away, finding refuge in some distant corner. What stood before her, what lay within her vision, was vibrant, unlike anything she had ever seen; seeming contradictions flowed deftly within and around lines of energy in a ballet so perfectly timed they created a mosaic. Within the mosaic an array of life forces intertwined, each one, while of singular purpose, interconnecting with the other. It was as if the universe was alive.

But that *couldn't* be. That was *impossible*.

Her entire life's experience hadn't begun to prepare her for such a moment. Life had always been here and now, and only here, and only for a select few, on one special planet shining within the firmament. The vision cascading before her was of a universe swarming with intelligence working on a vast scale, one that moved on a level that at times entered the realm of perfection.

There were benevolent personages, spiritual in nature, nurturing pockets of imperfection in a way that was quite touching; to what end, she had no clue.

Lost in the moment, the vision began to fade, leaving her dazed and confused, her concept of reality shaken to the core. From this strikingly new and different world there came into view, within the receding vision, yet another door. Through this one, though, light was streaming in an otherworldly glow. She saw, with growing fascination, there amidst the glow a shimmering visage moving through a blanket of stars, each one's reflection a different hue. The apparition touched the brightest one, turned slowly, and with an uncertain smile looked directly at her.

Then it was gone.

She blinked, completely flummoxed. Having no idea what would happen next, a taut sensation came from the part of her still clinging to the rock as the wind pressed her cheek. And the wind was something familiar, was something real, giving her comfort and a terrace upon which to rest. From her perch, she watched the last fleeting remnants of the vision disappear, and she took a breath. Though the workings of such mystery lay beyond her grasp, what had moved before her had been masterful, if a bit unsettling, and the echoes remained deep within as she negotiated passageways that led her home.

Once safely through the portal she felt a curious twist; the desire to return was instantaneous as was the recognition she could not. Shaking off the effects, she secured her position within a small crevice and saw the rock in a different light. His dull patina was still there, but underneath there lay a quality she had never noticed, a kind of luster, and she wondered about that, and she wondered why he had become silent. His gaze, though, while telling her there was no reason for concern, held the unmistakable look of one waiting for an answer.

The words "What do you see?" came roaring back into her memory, this time with no earthquakes or visions. Thankful for stasis, she took a moment and gave the question some thought, soon coming to the realization there was no real answer, or at least no really short answer. There must be some way to explain that to him without entangling herself in a long conversation. She thought about revealing what had just transpired but that could well lead to disaster, or at least some form of mild embarrassment. No, there was another way. She cleared her throat, and with the agility every raindrop possesses, asked her own question, thinking it might even be fun, now that she was feeling very much herself again, to begin with a tweak:

"We don't really think of you as slow. You would have to actually move to gain that status. I am a little confused, though, why you'd want to know what I see if you'll never get to go there . . . or go anywhere? Or is that it?"

She looked past him into the forest for a moment, not sure what to think, realization soon coming to bloom. "Oh! . . . Oh dear . . . I'd never thought of it like that, for Patricia's sake. Can't imagine how awful it must be to lie here forever looking at the same picture day after day . . . however do you cope?"

He took some time to think about this—not much time for a rock, but a very long time for a raindrop. So it was whimsy found its course. Having been through something extraordinary, and feeling a touch of sympathy for reasons she could not fathom, the raindrop's priorities shifted slightly. Not much, but enough to suppress the desire to move on. At the same time, the sun made an appearance, warming her in a way she couldn't resist. This may well have been the first time she was content to just be.

While the raindrop enjoyed her leisure, the rock began working on the implications. He found it telling that she thought he saw the same picture day after day. On the contrary: every day was a new day, and he had never seen two the same.

How different could a rock and a raindrop be?

The disparity of their thoughts showed no outward manifestation. Somewhere deep in the universe, though, messages were being sent to a select few: diverse beings whose dedication to universal progress had become legendary among their peers. They were beings whose work had cleaved, drawing them separately to scattered outposts within the vastness of time and space as life had slowly spread among the stars in wondrous and unthinkable ways. Ways only possible within divine accordance. They were emissaries of a higher order than is commonly known, and their joy was infectious, for they saw the universe from a different perspective. Now they moved in haste, for duty and for the prospect of seeing old friends. Soon they would gather in one specific place on one small planet to witness firsthand the momentous events about to unfold.

Chapter Two

The rock's focus had never been so much on what he saw, but rather upon the delicacy of interaction. Over time he had watched the world ebb and flow in the most exquisite manner. Discord would find the strains of harmony, then fall back into discord, only to begin again on some higher level.

His awareness began to sharpen, moving toward the horizon, taking in the valleys and roaming the gentle curves nature provides, searching for nuance, for connection, eventually finding within the delicate contours a slim thread from which to hang.

Making his way back, he stopped briefly from time to time, wondering what the chances were, and as his eyes fell upon the raindrop he saw for one small moment what could be if all went well. Electrons began moving in time to the possibility, began forming rudimentary plans for what could well be a moment that would burn into his memory, would become a part of the fabric of his being. He could feel the tide of life ushering him forward.

The raindrop returned his gaze once more, but hidden in her eyes lay a different story. She was wondering if she hadn't made a mistake. How long would it take him to answer a question like that? "However do you cope?" She hadn't even meant to ask it for Patricia's sake, there was just something in the moment. She was also wondering how life could become less than comfortable in such a short time. The sun was climbing higher, warming the world around her, and as steam rose, the thought of moving on began to weigh heavily. There seemed two options: slip quietly away, or stay for who knew how long until he thought it through. As the sun rose another degree, she slipped ever so delicately into a crease in his face, making her way toward a suitable departure.

His voice was low, rhythmic and commanding:

"What do you see?"

The raindrop froze, hanging precariously, knowing in all fairness she hadn't answered his question either. Refastening her grip, she began slowly and not particularly cheerfully, "Well, I really don't see as much as . . . experience." After a moment her voice tempered. "For the most part it's all a blur, everything moves so fast, and I'm never sure what's going to happen next. Sometimes, though, if I narrow my vision, things seem to slow down and I almost feel like I'm in control. For instance, when we make landfall, a decision has to be made whether to soak into the ground or try to make it to the river. That's of course if we make landfall, more often than not we make waterfall. Today though, when I leave your craggy curiosity behind, I'll be goin' to the river. You see, the forces that—"

"You've been in the river?"

"Well yes, we all go to the river at one time or

another, the difference being who gets where first, who bounces off what, that sort of thing. Providence aside, life for the most part, as far as I can tell, is not preordained. If there's a place I want to go, I'll see to it that a curve is negotiated just so, then head straight for a certain—"

"You've been in the river?"

"Why, is that surprising? We all end up in the river . . . we are the river."

"I've never been in the river."

"Oh, how sad, miss a ride like that."

The raindrop, realizing it may take longer than she had hoped, found her way to, and curled up in, a patch of moss. Relaxing within the luxuriant textures, she discovered, was a curious departure from her customary whirlwind dash for the lowest level on the gravity chart, and it was a rare moment that would allow for curiosity.

She had noticed while rolling over his surface that he was laced with markings worn and ancient. What a story they must tell, she thought, then shuddered visibly, knowing where that would lead if questions were asked; no raindrop could survive a tale like that.

She hadn't need for worry, though. The rock was still engaged:

"I may be a little slow here, but what do you mean, you *are* the river?"

"Oh dear, where do you think we all go in such a hurry?"

"Well, I see you go so many places."

"Oh, yes, of course. I can see how that would be confusing, and I see your point, but it is what we do: go places, everywhere, we go everywhere and help as best we can. Except for the deserts of course, it's hard to find volunteers. Actually, I was there once, and I can see why nobody wants to go back. Nasty little places. Although I suppose in a way they really are quite beautiful, just no place for a lady. But then, neither are the icecaps. Get caught in one of those and time takes on a different meaning. You know, when you think about it, ice caps aren't that much different from the deserts, what with the stark beauty and all. I suppose there's a lot to be said for stark beauty, but we prefer the river. We call it 'Raindrop Alley.' You have no idea how much fun a raindrop can have in a river: flowing with the currents, meandering effortlessly, finding old friends and comparing notes, then there's the one big moment we all prepare for . . . "

Her voice trailed off.

Almost every river she had been in emptied into an ocean. Explaining the complexities of that immense and divergent world was a daunting task, certainly beyond the range of her desire. But then, was that really what he wanted to know?

He wanted to know what she saw.

What an odd, tangled question.

She could no more answer that than explain an ocean, and thinking perhaps she had said enough, decided once more, luxury or no, it was time to go. When her grip began to loosen, there came a rumbling from the depths, rolling like distant thunder, reverberations reaching for what was left of the moment:

"Princess—may I call you that? Before you leave I just wanted to thank you for solving one of the world's great mysteries. My point of reference, of course. I can't believe I never got that. So that's where

the rhythm of the river comes from . . . I'll be darned."
He watched the puzzled expression as her grip ever so
delicately tightened. "I mean, I've never seen you actually enter the river in any great number, at least not in a
way that would account for the entirety of it all. I knew
you sort of moved in that direction, but then you seem
to move in a lot of directions, and I just never got that."

While giving thought to the peculiarities involved
in a seemingly simple matter, though he'd yet to
make up his mind about that, he was overtaken by
what was at the moment a staggering realization: it
was entirely possible raindrops might *even have names*.
"Where are my manners? Shouldn't be calling you
Princess as if we were friends, old and comfy like . . . I
mean, that could maybe, might be . . . um, rude . . . I
was wondering if, ah, if raindrops—"

"I'm . . . Reanne," she said with a touch of hesitation, not sure where this was going.

"Reanne." He rolled the sound off his tongue. A
fitting name for such an elegant creature. "Reanne, it
is pointless to tell you what laying here all these years
does to a—oh, by the way I'm Ignatius, please call
me Iggy—being such as myself. I wasn't always here
and I wasn't always this way. I have dim memories
of actually coming to rest here. What I did before I
could tell you, but I wouldn't know where to begin."
The raindrop gave an audible sigh of relief. "Let's
just say I've had a long time to watch the goings-on
around this one little corner of the world, and I can't
see where I'd see things being that much different
anywhere else. I tell you, Reanne, the universe is so
mystifyingly precise in such a random way, it's as if
someone is trying to tell us something."

The raindrop settled back into the moss. For a dull, ordinary rock whose greatest attribute was a flat face, he was beginning to show some interesting features.

"You're saying someone is serious about their playtime?"

"Yes. No . . . hmm, never thought of it like that. You have a . . . an *unusual* way of looking at things. Though, I don't think 'playtime' is exactly how I would phrase it. There's more to it than that, I mean there's so much more I can't even begin to scratch the surface. Don't even know if there *is* a surface. I do know that seemingly dissimilar events, more often than not, will ultimately unify in such a way as to create something extraordinary. One having nothing to do with the other, but here it is: the ordinary often becomes extraordinary simply by changing one's perception. There's a common thread there somewhere. Darned if I've ever figured it out.

"Have you ever noticed how a single blade of grass moves awkwardly back and forth? It's almost comical. But when a field of grass moves with the wind, it moves in patterns as close to poetry as I've ever seen. Have you ever noticed how colors, notwithstanding their individual beauty, almost always join toward the end of the day and follow the sun in the most spectacular manner? Where does the sun go, anyway? Why is it things always fall apart, then turn into something new just to fall apart again? Did you know that shadows will spend the entire day teasing one another and never say a word? Have you ever heard a shadow talk, or even whisper?" Reanne shrugged in vague acknowledgment as the rock pressed on, "I haven't either. I don't think they're real, but there they are. Everything moves in one subtle way or another, even the stars move. So many things move in a way that at first seems so disorderly, but if you watch long enough, it's all a dance, and a remarkable one at that.

"It's as if I'm the only thing that doesn't move, and it makes me wonder. I think there's a reason for all of this and I do my best to do my best to figure it out. I think I'm here to see it all from a certain point of view, and I think that whatever made this whole thing up wants us to see more than we see, so I'll ask you again."

"My, Iggy, you do go on." Her eyes roamed his expanse, her expression clearly skeptical. The rock's words were compelling, but beyond the range of her experience. *See more than we see. See more* what *than we see?*

This is the point at which, under almost any other circumstance, she would have left no matter how he tried to persuade her otherwise. However, the implications of her vision were beginning to manifest themselves. Iggy's version of reality had a certain allure. For the first time she had a desire, if only slight, to perhaps maybe look a little deeper into the complexities of existence.

Though she didn't quite have the hang of it.

"There may be something that made all of this, but I seem to have lost the feel for it. As far as I can tell, life just goes on. One day leads into the next. And what meager accomplishments we manage may be for reasons beyond my understanding, but I have yet to see enough evidence that would lead me to believe what you are implying, that we have some greater purpose. All I know is we end up where we start. Life is one big circle. I've been from one end of this world to the other, and may I let you in on a secret? It's a circle, too. It's all the same, everywhere you go, same old stuff."

She wasn't sure if Iggy was taken aback or not. It was so hard to tell with a rock; he lay there, apparently thinking, but what?

Iggy had taken it all in, remembering a time he, too, embraced the notion that this world held little more than a place to rest. He had been wrong, as was she. He knew from experience, though, that there was no way to penetrate the fog of her doubt unless there was a light from within. A light which emanated from the soul, illuminating the distant shores of promise. He wondered what the chances were that that light had ever shone within her, and he had no idea why he should care. But he did.

That thought led him down a well-worn path, one that had always shone with promise, perhaps not so different from those very shores. Many and often were the times he'd kick through the dust, hoping to uncover what wealth of perception lie buried, only to return home, his pockets empty. Now this small, delightful, thoroughly lost and misguided creature had nudged him in that direction, and he decided to travel the path one more time.

Dredging up old memories, he wandered through the years, back to a time when even he would be considered young, and looked on passively as the fleeting images made their case.

Reanne had no idea what was going on, but she abandoned any thought of leaving. A moment like this only came along once in a . . . come to think of it, a moment like this had never come along.

While the raindrop thought through Iggy's words, the rock continued to make progress. The images were coming much faster now. What was missing? He decided to try cross-references and traveled further back in time, studying the way the world had changed for good and for worse. *What current carried life forward?* he asked himself as the visions began to slow down. *No, that wasn't it. No, no, that wasn't it either . . . could be, but I don't think so . . . maybe if I . . . wait, what was that? Bring that back.*

Tumblers clicked, falling in succession.

A rock has no real way of showing excitement. Even so, some of the rocks around him seemed to shift slightly in their demeanor, as if they, too, felt his anticipation. Iggy paid them little attention, concentrating instead on this new perspective of a seeming contradiction he had unearthed years ago. At the time, it had been no more than a curiosity, but over time, the fact that it even existed had nurtured a sense of purpose and provided solace in his moments of doubt. He now saw a little more clearly the entanglements surrounding this paradox as it fell silently from his knobby but capable lips:

"If the natural course of the universe always takes the path of least resistance, why do we work so hard to understand what we don't know? Why do we go out of our way to go out of our way?"

Why indeed . . . tough one, he thought.

He knew, more often than not, an answer would emerge, shining through life's ever-present clouds. The clouds, as best as he could tell, were nature's way of saying, "Don't quit now, there's more." And it came to him that there was more, in a metaphorical kind of way—the nexus lay not in the paradox itself, but in the entanglements, whatever they turned out to be. They would clarify and emerge—*illuminating—shining from within* nature's very own clouds of mystery, revealing a bridge. Didn't matter where it went, was just nice to have one.

"Be darned, who would have thought clouds had that much to say? I wonder if this is what I think I thought it was? Seems we *go out of our way* for any number of reasons, but in the end, there is just one meaningful destination: the shores of promise, shores that are *illuminated from within* one's very own person. Well, okay . . . so that's it. The paradox will unravel itself on those distant shores . . . the shores of promise.

"But the promise of what?" he said in no particular way to no one in particular.

Working through the possibilities, he thought it best to go back to the beginning, and as he did so, a twinge worked its way into the lower levels of his consciousness. Resurfacing to find out why, his attention shifted abruptly—Reanne was quivering.

She had been reminiscing, her innermost desires guiding her inexorably back to the open door and the ethereal glow that fascinated her so, and peering inside, she'd found herself once more drawn into a foreign world. The intertwining of energies moved as before, but this time the lines of force were moving in a way that appeared to be language. As she attempted to decipher them, to her astonishment, she could see that they moved in a way that continually altered her depth perception, bringing her attention to a focal point, but from varying points of view. It was as if someone was attempting to explain to her that things weren't always as they would first appear.

She thought back to what Iggy had said: "I think that whatever made all of this wants us to see more than we see." Not sure what to make of that, there welled within her a desire to find how she had come to be in this odd but remarkable place.

The raindrop's voice trembled, filling the air in her lyrical way. "A long, long time ago, the idea that there was more to this world than the endless cycles seemed reasonable. I suppose I could go as far as to say unquestioned. Then somewhere along the line a kind of numbness crept in. Maybe I became jaded to the importance of the missions, or maybe I just lost my way in the confusion. Eventually I gave up, succumbing to the path."

"The path?"

"The path of least resistance."

Iggy's gaze flickered.

"Ever hear of it? Raindrops are real big on the path of least resistance. To us, it's a . . . well, a sanctuary."

She saw the rock's look of approval, giving her strength.

"Now Ig—may I call you Ig? To use your peculiar vernacular, I'm going to do my best to do my best to tell you what I see. I hadn't given thought to any of this in ever so long. When you asked such a pointed question, when you asked me what I saw, it triggered a flash, a sort of vision, and I didn't know what to make of it at the time, but now little bits are coming into focus.

"When I look out over the world, I see a vast panorama of things that for the most part I don't understand. I am Reanne, the insignificant and glistening." She saw the rock's shoulders ease and his face move toward a smile. "It hadn't dawned on me until a moment ago that some of what you say has a sparkle to it, that maybe you haven't been baked so hard after all. Memories are coming back, memories of talents lost. You see, there was a time when my eyes were, to put it the one way that makes sense, lenses. Lenses that opened the door into a larger world, focusing on complications that were really quite simple once the clutter was cleared and the distortions filtered out. Sad really, having lost that. But one never knows, do they . . . maybe someday I'll be . . . " Her face scrunched a little, then her voice became drenched in quiet disbelief.

"Wow, what was that? Oh dear Patricia, I can't believe this is happening. I believe the lens is beginning to work again, and I have to say, in a way . . . in a way that's much clearer and stronger than . . . oh, oh, and it keeps getting stronger. Oh my!

"Something just came into view, let me see if I can, hang on a minute, need a little readjusting here . . . well I'll be darned, who would have ever guessed? Ig, why is it we all get to see, and not only see, but each of us from slightly different points of view? How many of us are there? Countless! Think about it, it's mind-boggling."

"Ok, Reanne, I'm concentrating on concentrating and I think I'm with you. What you're saying is, if we didn't have eyes we couldn't see. And seeing as how we all look at the world differently and with varying degrees of insight there's bound to be . . . I have no idea what you're saying."

"Ok, Ig, follow me here. You said that there was more to life than meets the eye, and it makes perfect sense that you would be the one to notice something like that. After all, what else have you to do? So, with your help, it just came to me that we can all see."

"See what?"

"Whatever is out there."

"Whatever is out there. This is what you want to tell me, that we can see whatever is out there." Looking into the distance, he swore there would be no more talking to raindrops.

"No, seriously Ig, rework your focus and think about it. This world has more eyes than a river has reflections, and they all have someone behind them, some discerning intelligence. Wait a minute . . . what if we can see things because there are things to be seen? What an elegant balance that would be."

"You really are too much. Please forgive me, I feel a nap coming on." He was completely devastated. She had shown so much promise. Now this, going on with her senseless, inane . . . Damn!

His eyes took in the horizon as he yawned, settling in for what he fully expected to be the end of that.

Chapter Three

"No, wait, don't do that. How can you go to sleep at a time like this?"

Reanne could feel the moment slipping away, and that simply wouldn't do. A ripple formed at her core and moved outward, moved deliberately through the fluid lattice of her structure as it searched for the surface, once there exploding into energy. In tones no rock could remember hearing, she thundered, "Mr. Ignatius! You basaltic son of a bituminous boulder field, I am not finished, and you will hear me out!"

"Now what? I mean, what was I thinking? Asking one of these . . . vagabonds, that's what they are . . . little ragamuffins," he mumbled as his eyes carved the barest of openings.

"Oh, thank you. I couldn't tell this to anyone else. No one would, oh dear, I just couldn't leave until . . . " In her moment of pause, she couldn't help but think that for all his gruffness he was indeed a gentle creature.

"Iggy, you said that the world held clues to a greater intelligence. I would take that to mean that anything powerful enough to create all of this did so with a plan in mind and wanted us to be a part of it. So it came to me that in some ways we must be a reflection of whatever being took the trouble to make all of this. Think about it! We have the ability to feel and to care, to hear, wonder, communicate . . . and to see. For Patricia's sake, we even have the ability to create in a limited way, perhaps only limited by what we're willing to see. Maybe a force powerful enough to conceive and create infinity might have made all of this because it didn't want to be lonely, wanted someone to share infinity with. Did you ever think of that? Have you ever been lonely?"

Iggy was beginning to think he may have been a little hasty. She might take the long way around, but he could see the thread in her logic, and it was strong. His interest began to rise as did his spirit.

"Not really. I stay pretty busy," he said, untangling his voice. "Although, there are times when I, yeah, well, sometimes."

"Yeah, me too." Catching a glimpse of the river, she said, "Ever notice when you share something, you're not so lonely anymore?"

"Reanne, where are you going with this?"

"We are a reflection."

"We're reflections that can see?"

"No, silly. We are a reflection of the All-Seeing. We experience life in our own special way, look through our own tiny window, and share a limited but personal view with the Creator."

He repeated her statement over and over, each time a little louder as his derision melted away.

Searching for meanings, his eyes fell upon the river. And following the river he came to the horizon, and there beheld a panorama exquisite in its depth: one filled with uncertainties, hope and promise. What was out there, and what might come to pass? His thoughts overflowing, hanging in uncertainty, he made his way back, finding comfort as his gaze came to rest upon one particular tree. This tree saw the world from a different light, and Iggy was not unaware of the fact.

As he thought about the tree's interplay within nature, about the intertwining of things and events that had left their mark, a new question found its way into the landscape of his ever-changing world: *How could everyone be so very much the same and yet be so very different? What would cause that to happen, other than what Reanne had just said? We all looked from a window, reached out in our own way, hoping to touch some fragment of Divinity. What if the Creator was, on some level, a willing partner?*

He said with wonder in his voice, "If you could see through all those eyes."

"Yeah."

They stared at each other, contemplating the implications, allowing time to pass.

Eventually Iggy asked, "What do you think it would be like to see everything at once?"

"You mean see everything at once, as in comprehend all the viewpoints, feel what everyone is feeling, see the universe as the Creator *and* see it from the myriad pockets of creation in one giant vision?"

"Yeah."

"Couldn't begin to know."

Of course, how could anyone possibly know? The absurdity of his expectation brought him back to earth. And he felt the earth move. And in that moment a wall fell, revealing that which had so stubbornly remained out of reach.

He'd often thought there was an interconnectedness of realities—realities seen and unseen—and that there lay inherent, within the fabric of the universe, passageways that bridged the two. Reanne was a bridge. A startlingly fluid bridge. What had passed before him, however, was much more subtle. In that moment he had seen a way, the means by which one ascends to new spheres of possibility, and to levels of reality unimagined.

And it was so simple. Who would have thought?

"You know, Reanne, life isn't really a circle . . . it's a spiral."

This statement took a while to sink in. When it finally did, she saw that what lay within a spiral was promise and the latent power of progress. Within a spiral, *time* was involved in a way quite unlike that of the circle she had for so long seen as life's only purpose. Her imagination moved freely within the possibility that there was more to life than seeing one day to the next, that life held a significance beyond the idle comforts she had come to know.

Time, though, was something to which she'd never given thought. And it was most perplexing.

She tapped Iggy on the shoulder.

"Ig, do you think time is real or a phantom of perception?"

"A phantom of perception? Wherever did you come up with that? You're not really a raindrop, are you?"

"Come on, Ig!"

"Oh, all right."

This had come out of the blue, and a shifting of gears was in order. As he thought about it, it dawned on him that a straight line might be the shortest distance between two points, but he had never experienced the fluid world of a raindrop, and the nonlinear thought process involved therein. It appeared a straight line could miss things along the way, and he wondered just how much he'd missed.

"Those soft edges of yours are pretty sharp. Why do I get the feeling you've never asked another raindrop a question like that?"

"Ig!"

"Ok, okay. I'll tell you what I think."

He really didn't have a clue. It wasn't that he'd never tried to work the equation, it was just that the concept of time had always proven to be slippery. The sun reached its zenith before he had exhausted every possibility, and to his surprise, there was but one satisfactory answer:

"I think it is real *and* a phantom of perception."

"For not being able to move, you wiggle pretty good."

"No, really. Time's real in the sense that we experience its passing, but try and reach a rational concept and it plays a game. The more you try to pin it down, the more it slips away. Like trying to catch a shadow."

Reanne watched a wave of contemplation cross his face as they both thought it through. "Yeah, I see what you mean. What I don't get, though, is that a circle goes round and round and never, well, it's just that a spiral goes somewhere, kind of like time but in a different way."

"Makes you wonder where that somewhere is, doesn't it?" The rock paused, gathering the beginnings of a thought, then worked it through. "Reanne, how vast and complex is a universe that makes the lines of communication between us and the Creator so difficult to discern? I mean, we have all these clues, they're everywhere, but how does one even know where to begin? Hmm, maybe it doesn't matter. Maybe we should just listen. Listen and watch. Meanings do seem to reveal themselves over time. It's not that the communication isn't there, it's just so distant. You'll never hear some big voice say, 'Tuesday let's do lunch,' but Tuesday rolls around all the same. Know what I mean?"

"Not really, Ig."

"Oh. Yes, well, I suppose not, different worlds and all that." Iggy had a puzzled expression. How different could they possibly be?

"Maybe if I put it another way," he said, hope mixed in there somewhere. "No, better yet, I'll let you in on a secret, and this is just between us, okay?" She nodded.

"Okay." This he sort of half rumbled, not all that sure it really was.

"You look at a rock and think all is quiet and serene. Well let me tell you, the tension can be enormous. Things aren't always what they seem, and we can get a little insecure watching all this activity buzzing around. I've seen events unfold that would make your shimmer quiver. There are times I want to reach out and keep something from happening, knowing full well I can't. Then, just when I think all is lost, everything comes together, and quite often in the most astonishing way. One more revolution of the spiral. It's like a big, slow-moving revelation from some powerful force—food on the table, something to chew on, think about.

"The thing is, when you're in the middle of chaos it's hard to know how events will unfold, what forces are at work . . . what it all means. See what I'm saying?"

"Ig, I do believe you're falling off a ledge."

"Whoa, where?" He looked around furiously, checking the horizon, checking sensors for seismic activity, eventually turning to Reanne, his face melting into a sheepish grin. "Had me going there for a second. Ho boy, this is what I mean."

Reanne smiled the smile of a siren.

Over the years, Iggy had grown fond of his surroundings, and had spent an enormous amount of energy laying out the imaginary lines upon which he conducted his studies. To begin again at this stage in his life was disconcerting at best. In his moment of terror, a long-held notion of reality fell slightly askew: *What if this isn't my final resting place?*

The power generated by that possibility released memories of profound but difficult times. Iggy, along with his friends, neighbors and kin, had long ago become inundated by water, and the misery of their desolation had become unbearable, when a strange thing happened. A light began to flicker within each of them, a comforting light that came from the depths of the soul. Some could see it more than others, no one more so than Iggy, but the light became a friend, as if the hand of God moved among them.

Sounds came filtering in. "Iggy, where did you go?" The rock's startled look caused Reanne to burst into laughter. "Iggy, what are you doing?" she asked in a playful voice.

"Huh? Oh nothing, just thinking."

Plotting new bearings, he wondered if he'd begun to understand the delicate nature of a raindrop's world. While second thought told him he hadn't, gut feeling said he was close enough.

"Reanne, I want to tell you a story."

"Is this going to be a long story?"

"Ah, well, no." Actually it was a long story. It is doubtful any rock has ever told a story that was otherwise, but under the circumstances he would try to tighten it up.

"Way back when, we were a tight-knit group. Things were going swimmingly and we'd settled in, enjoying every day to the fullest. We spent time watching life evolve in the most curious of ways, wondering where it all would lead, certain only that a new world order was unfolding before us.

"One night there was a lively discussion as to the nature of our new neighbors when someone said, 'What was that, did you see that?' Well, nothing else happened that night, but it wasn't long until we all began to see it, night after night—long, flowing phosphorescent flashes. Within a few years, sound began to accompany the flashes and eventually the two became one—waves were crashing toward us. Everyone thought it grand because we were fairly high up. Beachfront property was what we all thought. Imagine our surprise when we discovered how brief that time would be. I have to say we enjoyed the moment, though. Nothing quite like the crash of a wave and that enchanting sound, especially when the day has gone and the wind with it. Nothing left but that sound.

"Next thing we knew, our dreams had been spent, all on what was not to be. We traded the beaches for the ocean floor. At first the experience was one of overwhelming joy. Marine life is so varied and spectacular. It flows in and out, up, over and under, proceeding all in a world of its own. Form, color, and movement came together in a way that altered one's notion of possibility, sometimes shockingly so. But all in all it was compelling, precise, and a thing of beauty.

"It was odd, though, to watch fundamental changes take place as the water deepened. Colors became obscure and the inhabitants less graceful—whole different world. As we sank further into the depths, conversations turned into questions like, 'Who was the last one to actually see a ray of light?' No one would answer, and desperation nearly overcame us. No one ever lost hope though, except some of the weaker sedimentary. We knew things would change. Even so, we were taken by surprise when change did come. One by one our senses shifted, and in the silence a strange thing happened. Over time, for a few of us, our thoughts began to echo. Well, not all of our thoughts, only the more profound and imaginative. Talking to each other squashed the effect, so those of us who found the phenomenon intriguing spent a lot more time thinking and listening, trying to figure out what it all could mean. Sad to say, everyone in that group has moved on. I'm the only one left. It is interesting, though, the way time brings meanings to the fore. Little by little a consensus grew within our small conclave: no longer hearing the sounds that once flowed so freely or seeing the beauty we so long took for granted, some part of us that had been dormant awakened. It was as if we could hear a voice within our souls calling to us."

Reanne, having no real confidence in the rock's definition of the word short, chimed in, "What did it say?"

"What do you see?"

"You already asked me that."

"No, I mean that's what it said."

"Oh . . . Oh! Oh . . . okay."

"A faint voice beckoned to us to dig deep and, for the first time in our lives, see the real meaning. Unfortunately we were all woefully inadequate and never really understood what the real meaning was. All we took away from the experience was a feeling. The only thing I have left from those days is the impression that infinity has living dimensions, and within them there is an intelligence that is infinite, that is ever progressive, and wants us to be a part of the adventure."

"So, you're saying infinity's imperative is to explore every possibility."

Iggy smiled and said softly, "Next thing you know, it's Tuesday."

Reanne returned the smile in a way that warmed Iggy's heart.

He became faintly aware of the rustle of leaves, the rush of the river, and the movement of beings not seen, as they, too, were in full discussion. *There are so many variations in life, and they have so much in common. A twist here, a turn there, that's all that separates them. Graduations within graduations,* he thought, *like stairways within stairways.*

"What did you say?"

Iggy was mystified. "I didn't say anything."

Shivers swept through the rock's fissures as Reanne said, "Graduations."

He searched her face as time stood still.

The raindrop turned abruptly and looked into the rock's eyes, her expression unreadable as she said half to herself, "Like stairways."

Iggy tried his best not to tumble over the precipice, but there was very little he could do. He drew on every concept of reality he had, found some he didn't know were there, and tried to claw his way back, but it was no use. He fell deep into recesses that had been undisturbed since he had last seen . . . what? Once fully submerged, he searched wildly for sanity and reason. *How could she have known that?*

After some time he began to regain his senses, reasoning that he had known early on there was something different about her, when a sound caught his attention. It was faint and elusive but unmistakable, a rhythmic echo that came from nowhere, not unlike the one he'd experienced so long ago, beckoning them all to see the real meaning. As he focused on the sound, he recounted those days of desperation and the light that had registered on some improbable level, a level transcendent, one far beyond the shores of promise he and Reanne so patiently sought.

At the time, he thought the light to be no more than a passing curiosity, and that he would never know such an experience again. Now the echo had come back, and he wondered if he would see once more that light—a light devoid of heat, lacking sharpness, and foreign to the eye, a luminescence visible only to . . .

Reanne had no clue where Iggy had gone, and that was curious, but no more so than the rhythmic pulse of life surrounding her. Moving slowly through the moss, she listened contentedly to the peculiar murmur rocks make when they're in a stir, the idle chatter of raindrops, and the occasional rub of branches as they, apparently uninterested, went about their business. It was all so soothing. Life was indeed mysterious, and she was glad.

Chapter Four

Iggy had known for a long time that there was a force moving inexorably along its path. Although he had never seen it move, nor did he have any idea what it was moving toward, he knew that its power came from somewhere deep in the universe and its purpose was change. Over the years he had documented the progression, bewildered by the precision of such might. And while he had always wanted to take a look at the workings, he'd never figured out how to engage in such an undertaking. Now he stared into the depths, and for the first time he could feel movement. There were no vibrations, no shifting landscapes, there were no signposts or rumblings, but change was in the air.

In the quiet of the moment the last echo was no more. And he thought about that. And he thought about Reanne. He had never met anyone who was telepathic, and he doubted she was. It seemed to him more likely that the forces he knew to be real, elusive as they may be, had manifested themselves in an uncharacteristic way. His guess was that it had something to do with the light. Answers lay within that light, of that he was certain, but how does one go about . . . Searching for points of reference, he laid out a preliminary grid, then began filling in the knowns, hoping to find a seam in the fabric.

The task proved to be daunting. After what seemed like days, desolation crept in. He was about to concede failure when he noticed that whatever was illuminating his world came from no particular place, nor did it register on a particular sense. What he was looking for surrounded him. Dismay intertwined with excitement as he examined his circumstance. Perhaps if all went well, the echo would return. Listening for the faintest of sounds, he heard nothing except a disquieting repetition of words that, to his surprise, were coming from his own mouth: "Spirit speaks of its own choosing—obliquely to material creation, directly only to itself. Listen to the living spirit within." Iggy closed his eyes, offered a silent prayer, and just before the explosion of light, he felt a peacefulness unlike any he had ever known.

Reanne had enjoyed her stay, but, as much as she wanted to continue their discussion, raindrops counted time differently. Iggy had apparently disappeared, and she had no idea if or when he would come back. Not entirely happy with the decision, she moved through the moss toward his edge, hesitating for a moment, hoping for a sign.

Had it not been for the moss, the shudder of his emergence would have thrown her irrevocably on her way. Managing to secure herself within the moss's matrix, she held fast and studied his demeanor, curious about the way he had resurfaced. He was silent and carried an odd expression. Careful not to say anything untoward, she began simply:

"Soooo?"

"Reanne?"

"Where did you go?"

"Reanne, it was there, I saw it."

Her outer edges twitched with anticipation and uncertainty, for he had become different in a way she would not have thought likely.

"What did it say?"

"Didn't hear words . . . there was a . . . an array, like a tapestry."

Iggy looked around briefly, preparing himself. "What I saw, I didn't see so much as I experienced. There were life forces intertwining in a way that approached perfection." He looked around again, hoping she wouldn't think him mad. "The universe is a structure that houses diversity—willful diversity."

Reanne's jaw dropped, and with complete wonderment in her voice, she said under her breath, "That's what I saw." Iggy didn't hear, though, for he was still entranced.

"Everything moved within levels, levels terracing from here to . . . to . . . does 'heights of harmony' sound a little much? But that's what it was . . . and grandeur . . . there was grandeur . . . grandeur and harmony in the far reaches. Within the levels I saw enlightenment, anticipation, and disappointment in every imaginable combination. There was a unity though. Everyone's aspiration leaned toward the same distant horizon . . . and lacing it all together were rings of . . . um . . . energy. The rings were linked in a simple unchanging pattern, like some kind of ordained unifier, independent and coming from . . . " The rock's vision sharpened. There had to be a source. Everything begins somewhere, and all those lines flowed within and between levels in a very particular way. His calm expressive voice became framed with awe. "There was a circuit, lines of force that emanated from, and returned to, the center of creation. I say that because I have no other explanation. But the lines were immense, flowing freely without pretense or prejudice. Interwoven was the most extraordinary thing, a form of energy that was there but it wasn't, a force in constant flux, as if the universe was thinking. No, no, it wasn't the universe. There were individual personalities. They were intermingling, expressing themselves, countless beings on countless levels of existence cradled in a loving hand."

Reanne said in the faintest of whispers, "*So what I saw wasn't a dream.*" And she, too, began to focus. What she had seen in the ballet of life forces was beyond her concept of reality. His version, though, not only presented a different view but created the curious effect of reinforcing her belief that the vision was a gift.

Iggy, unaware Reanne was making an attempt to reconcile what she had seen with what she believed to be impossible, pressed onward. "The levels contained ever-progressing correlations between living and nonliving energy forms, all moving within the auspices of pattern. There was unity in the midst of chaos. It was as if chaos was the raw material and some mechanism worked tirelessly to form some greater thing . . . some . . . oh my, can this be?" Bewildered in manner and spirit, he said in a hushed voice, "The patterns, they were the mechanism."

Completely overwhelmed by the discovery, his once-compelling resonance faded into silence. He had seen complexities beyond comprehension, all sharing one common thread—simplicity itself.

Reanne had hung on every word. Now there was only an eerie quiet. After some time she realized Iggy was finished, and she began hesitantly, "I have to say that what I saw was at times overwhelming, but in an odd way the beauty of it made sense, whereas what you're saying doesn't exactly. What patterns are what mechanism?"

Iggy had no idea where to begin. Perhaps something straightforward. "The mechanism was simplicity itself, it was pattern."

"Well that clears everything up. What are you talking about?"

He had seen pattern take on so many forms that explanation was entirely out of reach. All he could do was sigh and hope she would sense the magnitude of his challenge. As that somber moment stretched on, Iggy remembered seeing a phalanx of doors. Each door had opened into a realm controlled by a specific pattern, and the patterns held within became more complex and interconnected as the doors progressed down a line that fell into infinity.

All the patterns shared one similarity: while their purpose varied in near endless ways, they each confined themselves to a single unwavering function, which could only mean that, while they worked within the realm of change, they were themselves, each as a singular entity, *changeless*. What a wonderful system. All that *was* change worked within *unchanging* channels of unity. There must be a way to explain that to her. The first door had been the simplest, so he began there.

"Reanne, almost anything you can think of is defined by opposites."

"And that would include you?"

It was becoming apparent that, while she had a deep interest in their discourse, he wasn't making the slightest bit of sense to her. But that couldn't be helped. If he could come up with a way to keep her interested while his thoughts unfolded, he may yet win the day. He settled on a plan. "Okay, why is there a middle?"

"I can't believe you would say something like that. For some reason I thought we were having a serious conversation here. I really don't have time for this."

Iggy didn't move.

"All right," she said, still a little miffed, "I'll play one more round. There's a middle because there's something at each end. What's your point?"

"What would happen if there was nothing there?"

"Nothing where?"

"At each end."

"You really are trying my patience. If there was nothing there, then . . . " Her vexation turned to puzzlement.

Iggy had set the trap and she had fallen. He waited, hoping time would whet her curiosity. Finally she said in a small but firm voice, "Ok, Ig, you got me. What would there be?"

"Nothing."

"That's it. This is the last time—no more talking to rocks. One minute you begin to make sense, the next you're so far off the wall that—"

"The tension between the ends is the glue that binds. It's the tension between opposites that creates the dance in the middle. I think it has something to do with controlling the inner and outer limits of what's real. If it weren't for opposites there would be no middle and nothing could exist."

She would do one of two things: leave fuming, or stay, hoping to see where this led.

He prayed for the latter.

"You really are hopeless, aren't you? Would you mind explaining yourself before I go screaming into the night?"

"Reanne, why are there two extremes? Everything, or most everything, can be defined by two diametrically opposed . . . what would the word be? Oh hell, *opposites*. Everything from the negative and positive charges of physical energy, to the desires of personal pursuit countered by the whims of chance. The pattern never varies—two extremes, a whole bunch of middle.

"If it weren't for the fact that those boundaries had limits, nothing could exist because everything would keep falling further and further apart until there was no hope of interaction. Are those boundaries an accident? I would think otherwise.

"Reanne, how many things can you think of that are completely unconditional, that no matter what happens they embody absoluteness?"

"Well, at the moment, one thing comes to mind: I have absolutely no idea what you're talking about." Reanne had a look in her eye that told Iggy he'd better make this good.

"There may not be very many, but right off the top I can think of three: infinity, eternity, and certain aspects of reality. The first two don't even have boundaries, which makes them absolute in their own right. That last one though, that's the arena in which we all dwell. And I would think, as unlikely as it may seem, there are absolutes within reality, and pattern is one of them. The trick is finding what that has to do with us, which only requires a little thought. Well ok, in some cases, a lot of thought." Reanne's expression didn't seem to be changing. "Well okay, in most cases, a lot of thought."

She burst out laughing.

Iggy wasn't sure whether to feel hurt or laugh with her. Eventually she gave him a loving pat and said, "I really, truly, almost believe you have some idea of what you're talking about, but sometimes there are things that just don't translate. Try and remember I'm a raindrop, and take it from the top."

Iggy felt a flush of joy. "Your Princessness, if opposites are so very different, and we agree that they are, why don't they keep falling apart until they don't have to deal with each other anymore? Why do they insist on the dance? There must be an intelligent design that keeps everything within set boundaries. And it is a reality that the mechanism—the pattern of duality within nature—set up by that intelligence uses tension—the balancing of forces in opposition—as a means to hold everything together. Granted, there may be a great deal of leeway, but, ultimately, opposites can only get so far apart. There are absolute boundaries within aspects of reality, and nothing can change that."

"That what?"

"The fact that in the midst of chaos, nature, by and large, proceeds in an extremely organized manner."

Reanne was beginning to see what he was trying to say. She had to admit life had a certain undercurrent of orderliness to it, an efficiency that seemed natural and, quite often, invisible unless one searched for it. The realization shook loose something that had crossed her mind before Iggy had resurfaced.

"Ig, while you were wherever you were, I was cruising the moss and—are you listening to me?" He managed a nod. "Does 'mind is the realm of promise' mean anything to you?"

If there had been an earthquake at that moment he wouldn't have felt it. "That's it! You're a genius, my radiant little friend."

Reanne smiled the smile of someone who wasn't sure what had happened, happy all the same. "What does that mean?"

"I have no idea, but it's the key to all of this. What is at one moment crystal clear becomes increasingly blurred as events shift. That's the key: the confusion."

Iggy beamed.

"The confusion?"

"Yeah, the world is confusing."

"And this you call genius?"

"Well, you have to understand that just because I can't see the whole picture right now, it doesn't mean that what you just said is not an important part of the puzzle and that you're not brilliant. But it's a perfect example. In order to see the bigger picture, you would have to see the entirety, one end to the other, right? Most of the time we can't see the ends because we're so caught up in the middle."

The derision in her voice could have wilted sand. "We can't see the ends because we're in the middle. I knew no good could come from this. We can't see the ends . . . because . . . for Patricia's sake! What next, some cockamamie story about circles having opposites? No wait, let me guess. How about circles begin and end somewhere, or maybe—"

Iggy's smile brought a sudden halt to her tirade. She sat and steamed until exasperation took over, and she finally said in a tightly clipped voice, "What?"

Iggy hadn't intended using the "circle has ends" example because there were larger issues at work, such as the fact that a circle only had ends if there was a natural starting point, which was not always the case, or if it took on the astoundingly wonderful dynamics of a spiral, a concept he was in the process of trying to more fully grasp. But as long as she'd brought it up, perhaps he'd better go in that direction and steer back on course somewhere down the line.

"Reanne, that impressively gnarled and rather imposing structure standing next to us is a legend around here. He's lived longer than any tree we can remember, and we remember a lot. Every other tree you see is either his offspring or the offspring of someone he knew. There is a quality about Barkmoore. I'm not really sure what it is, but energy flows strong in him.

"Wasn't always that way, though. In the beginning, trees had some pretty odd habits and they didn't seem very bright. We weren't sure what to think of them and saw little hope things would get better. But, turns out we were all—tree, grass and stone—working toward a common goal, something no one would have guessed.

"You see, before his forebears took over this part of the world, we had been used to a tidy, uncluttered way of life. Even the grasses of the field held court with a sense of reverence. Then leaves started showing up, and we weren't sure what to make of them until the source, over a period of time, marched in from beyond those ridges. In our time frame it was as if they came blowing in here like a whirlwind; nevertheless, they started throwing pieces of themselves wherever and whenever they darn well pleased.

"What you see standing so elegantly before you now was no more than a nuisance, to our way of thinking. The relentlessness began to fester deep within us. I mean, they were downright rude. We never said anything, but I think they knew how we felt. Didn't seem to bother them, though. What really curled my crust was the once-a-year special when everything cut loose, leaves flying everywhere, couldn't see a thing. Then to make matters worse, you ragamuffins would come along and cement the deal.

"One morning I felt the heat of the sun raining down and was desperate to see something—anything. That was the morning I decided to grow up. Harboring ill will had never proven to be an effective problem-solving technique, so I thought perhaps I'd try a different tack."

Reanne began to steam again. "This is going to be another long story, isn't it?"

If Iggy heard her, he didn't let on. "I took a mental journey, reliving the dark times, feeling the cool damp of the ocean's depth, trying to remember exactly what had happened there. It took some doing, but the effect was well worth it. Having found attitude, I was working on pitch when I thought about the way trees bend in a breeze, not unlike the grasses of the sea when they sway in the currents, and it all came together: lose yourself in the world instead of fighting it. See why things are the way they are, rather than passing judgment. So once the leaves blew away, I began to watch what was going on. Year in and year out I began to notice cycles. Cycles of creation and cycles more difficult to define. But there was always some form of progress, whether it was within myself or in the way life around me became more unified and tolerable. The cycles would repeat themselves, and there was always that one unique moment when you knew you'd been there before, only now was better. You see, circles do have beginnings and endings. It all depends on where you stand, what you're willing to see.

"One brilliant shining day it all became so clear. The forest had no interest in being rude; it was just nature's way of moving forward, not only for them, but for all concerned. Isn't that right, Barks?"

His only answer was a faint rustling of leaves.

Reanne's shimmer fluctuated within the currents of mystery, for at that moment *there was no wind.*

And that gave her pause.

She looked from the tree to the rock then back to the tree, and thought for a moment, then turning back to the rock, her expression melted into a softer, kinder, almost rueful contemplation. "So then . . . what you said about chaos being the raw material and not being able to see the ends because we're so caught up in the middle?"

"Slowly I began to notice the precision with which randomness works. We have a hard time seeing it because our horizons are so limited that what appears chaotic on one level is a work of art on another. The trick is seeing the big picture, locating the opposites. From that perspective, things are actually quite orderly, like blades of grass moving in the wind."

"I see what you're saying, but what does that have to do with my question?"

"What question?"

There was a pause as she gathered every bit of decorum she could muster. "The realm of mind, promise. Why did that make your sand shift?"

Iggy began working on the complexities created by the simplicity of opposites. Specifically, how mind could transcend the material while remaining a slave to nature. He was missing a very simple point, or was it too complex? Had to be one or the other. He wanted to answer her in a way that was concise yet managed to suggest the immensity of the depth. Problem was, he had become trapped by the quandary and could see no hope of disentanglement.

Chapter Five

Reanne was becoming used to the rock's penchant for internal discussions. Dismissing the impulse to pass quietly toward the river, she moved slowly through the moss. What she had in mind might require a little temerity, but the effort could prove worthwhile.

"What do you think about all of this, Mr. Barkmoore?"

Fully expecting him to remain silent, she thought about what the rock had said and she reflected upon meanings. Coming to no real conclusions, she made another attempt to entice the tree into conversation, hoping he might be able to shed light on the rock's pronouncements.

"Surely you must have an opinion. I know you've been listening, and you're probably smarter than the rest of us put together. I've visited your kind before. You pretend not to notice us, but sometimes we hear you talking, and it seems we're your friends. Tell me what you think."

"I think you talk too much." With that, he turned his leaves to the sun. No one noticed the faint beginnings of a smile.

"Well that leaves you and me, Ig . . . well, me, anyway." Her voice had an edge that reached into Iggy's core.

Shaken from his reverie, he looked around. "What? Huh? Oh. What, you think he'll just . . . I don't know . . . tricky stuff that, getting a tree to talk," he finally rumbled.

The raindrop gave him a "you don't know very much about trees, do you" look.

Iggy showed no outward surprise, but he wondered just what this enigmatic creature was up to. Deciding to take her lead, the rock began thoughtfully, "He's really a clever fellow. A lot of what I've learned he's hinted at, but never said straight out. Sometimes I think about it. He's in a unique position: roots that grow deep, a strong but supple trunk, and that crown of his. Can you imagine what it must be like to see from way up there?"

It took her a moment to realize he was serious. "Well . . . there is that possibility."

"Oh, of course, how silly of me." He said this as his eyes returned to the tree, roaming the contours and textures. "He's friends with the wind, the sun, the ground . . . " Iggy looked back to Reanne. " . . . and you. Like I said, he's special, but I'm not sure how. Never known him to talk much, at least not to us. There are no wasted words though; gets right to the point, he does. I think we try to figure things out he already knows."

Reanne's vision moved from the tops of Barkmoore's massive roots. Exploring his slightly irregular trunk, she came to the first divergence. Two more trunks half the original size continued upward, each

branching yet again. As her eyes followed one particular section, the branchings became more common. She soon discovered that the mechanism of his
expansion was extremely ordered and quite predict-
able. Oh, there was the occasional rogue coming off in
some irregular manner, but, by and large, his branches split off two by two. She followed another section
and yet another until her eyes pulled back and took in
the fullness of his magnificent crown. All that beauty
from one simple pattern, she thought to herself. Staring into his canopy, something the rock had said came
back to her: "One having nothing to do with the other,
but here it is: the ordinary often becomes extraordinary simply by changing one's perception." She studied the tree as he stood there in all his majesty, an occasional drop falling from his loft.

"Mr. Barkmoore, sir." Her voice was silk, negotiat-
ing a thin line this side of offense. "Could you tell us
what you see?"

It was a bold move.

The tree's massive circumference moved slightly
in the wind, leaves fluttering independently at varying altitudes. Barkmoore had taken an interest in this
most unusual of conversations from the beginning.
However, the thought of actually joining in had never
occurred to him. Interchanges under extraordinary
circumstances had been known to happen—a side
here, a bit of chatter there—but a full philosophical
discussion?

Barkmoore was borderline as to whether this was
such a moment. The tree knew it was not in a raindrop's nature to be so forward, but the fact that she
had gone out of her way intrigued him. He searched

for reasons to remain silent and found many. He would have to be careful at first. Make it simple. And there would be complications: translations that wouldn't come out quite right and meanings that would be lost in the mix. He could think of many other reasons, but mostly, it just wasn't done.

Scanning the horizon, he wondered what freedom was like and what mysteries lie beyond the limits of his vision. He wondered what joy solitude could bring . . . and what could make her so bold . . . and the balance tipped.

No one noticed winds ushering forth from afar, nor did they sense the Gathering.

To Iggy's delight, Barkmoore began moving his branches in a curious manner. Leaves wiggled in odd ways, bark shifted against bark, and an occasional twig fell to the ground, bouncing lightly off the carpet. The same peculiar behavior began moving in waves throughout the surrounding forest, rolling with a sudden gust of wind, moving outward into the distance until there was complete silence. Though Iggy could feel something was about to happen, he was unprepared for what would come next.

With a flourish the tree's whisper rose to pitch. "You two are tearing me up!" His laugh slow and boundless. "Where does one begin with no end in sight, eh? But then, perhaps that's the joy, no? Yes? What you really want to know can't be found by dissecting enegerial flow, although I have to admit it is fun to do that.

"Opposites, you say? Beginnings—always a good place to start. Don't mind sayin' you're a bit shy of the wicket, though. A twist inside a turn around the bend is a place to be found if one were so inclined—the beginning of the beginning of one thing with the other.

"Hmm."

There was a silence as the tree gathered his thoughts—Iggy and Reanne stood in rapt attention, awe of the moment pouring forth.

They hadn't long to wait, for the tree moved easily within his stately rhythm.

"If one *were* so inclined, the true nature of the universe *is* to be found. However, one must first understand reality. And while, as with time, it is difficult of definition, a great many things can be learned by watching reality bend to the Creator's will. We see so little, and there is so much. Tell me we aren't here to see more, to see what part spirit plays in the material world. Iggy knows this, but he doesn't know why. The clues are subtle, like pieces of a puzzle."

Iggy blinked.

"Think you discovered math because you learned how to count? How long do you think a language like that has been around? What other language pervades the universe by command, works tirelessly within pattern, peers from every corner, and, on occasion, reaches beyond, laying the groundwork for new frontiers?

"We take so many things for granted because our reference points pale, because time is older than are we. In youth it's not unusual to be uppity, to howl at the moon and parade brashness with ease, flaunting talents untempered. But as you so eloquently put it, Ig, there are two very opposite opposites. Discovery is a marvelous journey, but journeys take time, and time can be a stern taskmaster. Somewhere along the way, chance dictates a long hard fall."

Reanne tugged at Iggy and said under her breath, "Wow . . . and I thought you were longwinded." She looked from Iggy to the tree then back to Iggy, whispering, "You get the feeling he's not talking about the weather?"

Once more, Iggy took his cue. "Barks, what was that about reality bending? I thought it was a straight-line kind of thing. I mean it either is or it isn't, right?"

"Right? Huh. Right. You know from your dealings with our radiant little friend here what a straight line can do. If we're talking pure geometry, it's a good bet, but life isn't pure geometry. The shortest distance between two points in life's various journeys has to take into account the unexpected challenges found within any given situation. It's that way on purpose: dilemma steels the mind, embracing difficulty strengthens the spirit. Did I hear you say we couldn't see the ends because there's so much middle? Intriguing, don't you think? You have an inkling, but let me tell you, it is more fascinating than you could possibly imagine. Every day we are given the opportunity to observe reality as it wends its way through nature's palisades. Ever wonder why heat always rises, or why our little friend here stores latent energy when she turns to ice?"

Iggy looked from Barkmoore to Reanne, a bit perplexed. "Latent energy? I . . . ?"

"It's a buffer, a way of slowing things down. Makes the world more orderly."

"Oh, how clever."

Turning back to the tree, Iggy began to settle in, sort of.

Barkmoore watched as the rock struggled with meanings beyond his range and decided it was best to use examples more fitting, if somewhat esoteric. "Ever wonder why good ultimately triumphs over evil? 'Tis because evil has no real power. It is no more than a temporary distortion swirling around those who choose to elevate self over the well-being of others. Even so, good will find a way to utilize such unfortunate manifestations to further its cause.

"Think about the way harmony brings us together, the way equality creates calm and prosperity. What has arrogance and self-importance ever done for anyone? Who has ever rejoiced over the wonders of betrayal, or raised voice in song to some bit of treachery? Patience, fairness, a kind deed . . . you see what I'm saying?"

They stared at him in silence, thoughts bending in ways neither had expected. It seemed reality as seen by a tree took on added dimensions. Even so, the rock and the raindrop had been a part of nature from the early days and had experienced in their own way, and in varying degrees, the truth of the facts presented before them.

While Reanne took solace in the wisdom the tree had displayed, Iggy was consumed by an overwhelming thought. Having spent a good portion of his life working on, and fine-tuning, philosophical complexities, he held in his treasury a wealth of information from which to draw, and now this tree had stirred the pot.

The notion of a tree so freely and so easily *revealing* his contemplations sparked a convergence of two other, perhaps oddly paired, but long-simmering notions—the worlds of shadow, and *revelation* from on high. He had long been aware that a shadow was exceedingly shy and not one to converse in such a manner. He'd come to understand, however, that shadows had their own special place in the scheme of things, other than providing a cooling shade. They could and would *reveal*, with a certainty, if and when anything of substance was present. So it came to him . . . maybe they have something to say after all, in their own inscrutable way. Could it be that simple? He wondered if that's what Barks was trying to—

"So, you're saying reality is the Creator's shadow?"

"Bravo!" Leaves flung together, smacking in the wind. "Perhaps I've misjudged you. I think I'm beginning to see what the raindrop is up to. Part of it, leastways."

The tree looked out over creation toward the horizon as words fell quietly, "Knowing how raindrops can be, this is only the tip of her 'berg."

Barkmoore stood there in all his glory, energy transforming relentlessly, leaves skillfully cleaving light into verdant hues. His gaze shifted from the horizon to fields scrambled in a random sort of beauty— saffron, taupe and amber. Venerable fields laced with forested fingers of emerald, sage and malachite. He marveled at the balance held within the relationship of forest and field, and he wondered how such a thing had come to be. Who had found pleasure in creating this primal interaction, had set in motion curiosity without end . . . and why would Reanne, of all creatures, a world traveler, want to know what he saw? The tree's curiosity moved with purpose and determination, traversing the forest's shadow, passing familiar sights until coming to rest fully on the raindrop.

Reanne returned his gaze, unflinching, taking his interest to heart. A great deal of information passed between them: some of it clever, some interesting, some at times elaborately sequenced, even uplifting, but nothing that would pass for revelation. Finally the tree understood. Whatever secrets lay within her soft exterior would stay there. Resignation turned his attention back to the rock.

Reanne closed her eyes and drew a breath.

Far-off winds swirled and settled as if making a landing. In their midst, apparitions one by one appeared. They moved with ease, delight filling their countenance. In the background, dark-blue and steel-gray plateaus, suspended luxuriously, lumbered slowly toward the horizon, their pure white blooms expanding upward—monuments to the receding storm. No one paid heed to the sun as it moved just under the speed of recognition, save a select few, their voices joined in hushed expectation; the Gathering almost complete.

Chapter Six

Iggy was oblivious to what had taken place between the tree and the raindrop. He was, however, not completely unaware of the tree's shifting concentration and he would have paid more attention, but his newfound concept of the way the world worked was just beginning to settle in. The implications of being merely a shadow cast from some greater thing, at first tended to diminish the value of existence. Then again, he thought, it could mean we are all an intimate part of something wonderful. If that were true, if the material world was the Creator's shadow, what kind of being would cast such a hue? All he could come up with was something brilliant, powerful, and pervasive. He turned his eyes toward the tree.

"Barks, would I be wrong if I said that we are in some way partners in creation, in the unfolding of a universe?"

"You do continue to amaze me."

"Well, am I wrong?"

"No, my friend. You get the idea."

"So how much of us is shadow and how much is real?"

"I don't think you can quantify it like that. It's not that you're actually a shadow. It's more like, oh gosh, think of it this way: The physical world is the manifestation of the Creator's desire to share. As partners in the unfolding of a universe, the ultimate journey is, for us, the search for what is real, what the Creator wants to share and why."

"Ok, I'm lost again. I mean, how would you even begin a journey like that?"

"Ahh. That is the heart of it, isn't it? And it's not easy. But, discovery is a powerful thing. It brings into focus the various facets of existence. We view the infinite through the finite, and we have to work within those constraints. We are shadow in the sense that, while spirit is eternal and unwavering, the material is transient, raw, and ever in flux.

"Didn't I hear our little friend here say we're reflections of the All-Seeing? Think about that. Where lies the difference between reflection and shadow, eh?

"Tenuous though we may be, a heart should be filled, for we are blessed with the exhilarating, albeit confusing, often difficult task of finding equilibrium and discovering the higher meanings in life through experience. Seems there's something about learning the hard way that leaves a lasting impression. I suppose if we're going to be around for a long time, lessons have to stick."

"Excuse me, but what would you know from a long time? I mean, you guys drop like flies. I just get used to one of you being around, and you pop off like it was nothing." Iggy's brow furrowed. "Like that's the way it's . . . supposed to . . . I'm missing something here. You want to tell me what you could tell me that you aren't telling me?"

"You do get to the point, don't you? Ig, have you ever wondered why there are so many stars?"

"I suppose because there's so much room."

The tree laughed, searching for words. "Imagine how much energy is out there that we can see. How much more do you think is out there that we can't?"

"Yeah, I've thought about that. The probabilities are probably . . . whoa, wait. What kind of 'more' are you referring to, and what does that have to do with . . . ?"

"My crusty companion, search deep within yourself. See what happens."

Once more the rock dove deep for answers, his face showing determination as the last of the Gathering moved into place, inching closer to witness the spectacle. Iggy's furrow began to undulate, his eyes looking into the reaches of space, searching. Finally he said, "A vacuum will pull into it that which is necessary."

Barkmoore was beginning to understand some of Reanne's frustration. "I'll go out on a limb here and assume you have a reason for saying that."

"Yes, yes I do. I'm curious. If there's a lot of energy, and a lot of space out there, I'm wondering about placement. What exactly is the mechanism that causes the shift? At some point a thing has to be done, or a decision has to be made. At what point do events conspire to cause something to go one way rather than the other? Think of the combinations. How can it be so simple yet so complex? I just don't get it. Does a vacuum pull into itself that which is willing, or that which is required to fill the void?"

"Are you sure you're a rock?"

"Oh, come on, Barks."

"It is a delicate balance, I'll give you that."

Iggy was lost in thought for a moment, rebounding with a quiet, "What *is* out there?"

Barkmoore didn't answer, but the rock could feel a tremendous amount of activity underground. Signals were being sent in rapid fire, and some of them were particularly intense. Iggy had begun to wonder if he hadn't overstepped his bounds when the vibrations came to a sudden halt and the tree prepared to speak once more.

"Seems some of my associates were in disagreement. I pointed out that there should be nothing to fear by speaking the truth. In the end no one could argue with that.

"There are things between us that remain tantalizingly unsaid, and in the spirit of the moment, I am tempted to say more than perhaps I should. This much is clear: you're missing the bigger picture. Whether something goes willingly into a vacuum is of little consequence; the point is that there is movement."

A pleasant breeze blew through Barkmoore's branches as he considered how much more he should say and in what manner. Without a set agenda there was no telling where this could lead, and his friends had stated their concerns. But Iggy's interest was compelling. So it was the tree began.

"Consciousness is a curious thing, neither encroaching nor consuming. It is either there or it isn't. Intelligence is a different sort of animal, existing in varying degrees and on infinite levels. One is born of the other in a tightly woven embrace, having little in common save the need for each other's survival. We may never fully understand the dynamics of such an alliance, but one thing is certain: we are here, and we are aware of such a fact.

"The fact that we are aware of being aware should tell us a great deal. First, that we have something to be aware of, and that something is aware of us. Then, that there is a plan at work in such a way. Don't you find it curious that life is inextricably bound on every level to the laws of dynamics, to loss and gain? Even the worlds of thought and desire cannot escape such a force. While the laws of dynamics may well appear to captain their own ship, they are merely tools, extravagant sentries to the world of order—a level buried within a level: the level of verity."

The tree looked from one to the other, taking his time, for what came next was more than a leap of faith; it was, to some, a matter of deduction. "What you saw in your moments of clarity, each of you, will bear this out. The physical laws of creation are designed and controlled by intelligence, which should give you insight into the complexity and scale of the universe, not to mention the scale and complexity of said intelligence. It is easy to think that what we can't see doesn't exist, but laziness and ineptitude—now there are cruel masters.

"You have seen small slices, faint and obscure clues to the puzzle. Whetted your appetite, spurred you forward, didn't they? Stimulated your desire to commune with the cause of creation.

"I would think we could all agree that the lack of verbal communication with intelligence greater than our own hardly implies nonexistence of that intelligence. Understanding the workings of higher mind is limited by the constraints inherent on any given island of awareness, by the level of intelligence within any given personality. It is a safety valve. Maturity takes time. Limited knowledge can be dangerous, but in the wrong hands, in the hands of an imperfect being . . . " Barkmoore stopped short as he watched the rock's face glow with the beginnings of comprehension.

"Unlimited knowledge would be disastrous." Iggy finished the sentence, for this was a concept with which a rock was familiar. Knowledge is best gained layer by layer; vistas opened on each new level, and what was learned held varying degrees of value, the overall growing with the interlacing of wisdom and forbearance.

Leaves fluttered gently as the tree embraced Iggy in a thoughtful stare, then spoke with ease. "There is a pliant working relationship between even the most diverse frontiers. And while higher mind does not seek to control individual decisions nor prevent less than fortunate circumstance, don't you find it curious how unfailingly providence conspires on the side of propriety?"

Iggy looked up and said to Barkmoore quietly, "There are always impressions left by the footprints of perfection."

For the first time Barkmoore moved uneasily. "I'm wondering here, is this rather staggering insight of yours the culmination of study or of experience?"

"Study? Huh? Oh, no . . . no. Um, Barks, sometimes I can see the bigger picture, but then it is always framed by an even bigger picture, and I feel so small. Well, sometimes it all seems so hopeless. But then I think there is always hope, so I go on studying. Hmm, must be study, although experience certainly helps."

Reanne shook her head, laughing.

Iggy laughed with her momentarily, but he was still puzzled. "I have to say that what I saw in—I don't really know what to call it—wasn't so much a vision as an opening of doors. What the doors open into I have yet to figure out, but I saw something, and what you're saying is what I saw." He looked at the tree in a way the tree had never seen. "What did you mean, 'how much more energy is out there that we can't see'? What kind of energy?"

Swaying slightly in the wind, Barkmoore felt the strain of roots deeply anchored. It was a faint pull, just enough to adjust his appreciation. Life was indeed mysterious, as was Iggy surprising. He chose his words carefully:

"The power of discovery is not material in origin, so what does that tell you?"

Iggy took some time to think about this, finally uttering with a quiet assurance, "It is orchestrated by spirit."

"I am impressed." Feeling the dampened earth, Barkmoore noticed how easily energies flow, and how elusive the process was, not unlike his effort to define something intangible. "There is a caterpillar making its way just within your view. What do you see?"

"I see a caterpillar."

"Nothing more? What about destiny, what tomorrow will bring? Do you not see that wings will take flight?"

"Oh, well yes, but . . . what are you saying?"

"This young creature has no more idea what is to come than do you."

"I have wings?"

"No more than a shadow, unless you seek what is real within you. We may have material origins, but they are the framework from which to fly. Our work, simply put, is to follow where truth may lead, and in truth, make an ever-expanding attempt to find harmony, to fuse personal will with that of the Creator. Once allied in such a manner, distortions fall away, limitations become insignificant, and fear finds precious little to cling to. Gives new meaning to the word 'power,' doesn't it? And where do you think the source of that power lies?"

A bit of sand, finding purchase on the rock's ledge, teetered momentarily then tumbled free. Iggy's eyes flickered, his thoughts racing as the tree forged ahead.

"For some reason we find it difficult to fathom the simplicity buried quietly within the laws of inverse proportionals—a level within the level of dynamics. Lust for power is a highway to extinction, while the search for truth, for fairness, is ever-empowering. Reanne knows what I'm talking about, though you'll never get her to admit it."

She feigned indignation.

Iggy gave her a glance then looked back to the tree. "Well, yeah, I can see how that would work. But why is everything so hard to see? I mean, it's all so hidden. Why can't we just . . . I'm confused."

Barkmoore showed no sign of concern. "What we see here is in many ways *pattern*, a reflection of the larger universe. Our misconception is that we are somehow the board from which all life springs, when we are clearly not. Levels within levels, isn't that what you saw? The universe is far too vast for this to be the crowning glory of it all. We are certainly a part of it, but no more important than any other jewel in creation. That we can't see the higher workings is by design, but as blind as we may be, there are always clues, traces left by the execution of a plan—or have I misquoted your primal ponderance?"

The tree appeared to become lost in thought for a moment, then, gathering momentum, he said, "When events unfold in ways that seem decidedly unfair to one over another, or in the short term favor evil over good, I think that these inequalities should tell us a great deal. Perhaps they should tell us more about what we have yet to achieve than any misplaced notion of a Creator's indifference. What is paramount in the universe is the primacy of freewill, even if, on this level, not much goes smoothly at first. It all seems so hard because what is to be gained by the struggle is far too important to be given freely." Closing his eyes, Barkmoore's branches swayed with majesty as he contemplated the enormity of this simple truth.

Iggy had listened to the words. Now he stood on the brink of comprehension. In a world rife with misunderstanding, how much was actually what it seemed? Looking back, he found little to regret except the never-ending questions that haunted him so. Now, that regret began to dissipate. He was beginning to see that understanding was more a reference point than a destination.

The raindrop's warm embrace and the affectionate effort of the tree's desire to impart knowledge was a new and satisfying sensation. He began to reminisce, began working the tree's words into what he'd come to know and trust through a lifetime of experience. Shuffling through his layers and winding down various corridors, he eventually came upon that mystical and mysterious stretch of gem. He loved this place. He loved it for many reasons. That light would, on occasion, seep through and shine on hidden plateaus of perception was chief among them. As he descended through the plane, electrons stirred, moving into alignment, and he saw the world suddenly, clearly, and simultaneously through various facets. Formerly disjointed bits of information came together, forming a picture, and a portion of that picture had a curious wrinkle. In his review of the preceding moments, he saw how Reanne had moved slowly in the moss without saying a word. And when Barkmoore mentioned that she was aware of the inverse proportionals, she had refused to admit it, though she must have known all along. It seems Reanne was not as naive as she let on, and for the moment, she should not know that he knew.

This realization opened a new door. Crossing the threshold, he tossed his harness and began to travel, searching for something from the past that would illuminate the present. It wasn't long until he lost sight of home and found himself moving through time without restraint, sometimes becoming lost within terraces that struck his fancy. He thought back to a time before trees, before these wonderful creatures had come to dominate the land, before the grasses of the field, before anything moved but the wind and whatever it pushed. Visions of sand swirled, sand moving in patterns wholly uninterested in any form of discipline save complexity. But patterns emerged, simplified and discriminating, and in time patterns repeated, laying the groundwork for his successive attempts at confirmation—something momentous was afoot.

Over time, sand and wind worked together, re-shaping familiar outcroppings into sculpture, breath-takingly beautiful sculpture. Children were born— new outcroppings flaunting elegance and youth tow-ered majestically, hoping to age gracefully. Iggy had been there watching the earth change, small subtle changes, large cataclysmic changes, all made in the name of progress, and there was nothing he could do to alter any of it. He was a passenger on a flight to the future.

What's the very first thing you remember, he asked himself. *What's the first thing that registers on a conscious level? Well, I vaguely remember pressure, then a series of vibrations, there was shifting, a lot of shifting and a lot of noise, then I remember seeing . . . light. Long, angular, heat-inducing light. Brilliant, warm, "there's work to be done and I hope you enjoy the ride" kind of light.*

So let's take it one step further. Where did the light come from, its power shining in such a manner? What unimaginable being created a stage, wielding a mighty scepter, and set the heavens ablaze with stars beyond count? What kind of force would find that easy to do, and what kind of entity would create things, then share with that which was made, according to their desire and capacity?

What kind, indeed!

Ok, those questions are unanswerable, but then you knew that. Let's bring it a little closer to home, see what happened when all that happened. One thing that happened for sure was

*the emergence of opposites. Said entity created opposites in a
way that allows for definition and limitations within which
boundaries can be set, thereby creating a playing field. On,
in, and around that field there were put, placed, and flung, a
lot of round things, some giving off, some receiving energy:
an interaction that spills the word "opposites" all over the
place. And to make all that work, said entity sprinkled in a
wee bit of space to separate and to insulate . . . then there's
my very own, my very best and treasured friend, the one
and only, the inimitable, and the peerless . . . Father Time.*

Time and Space . . . lot goin' on there.

In a lot of ways.

Darn lot o' ways.

*Wonder what they'd be, though . . . one without the other.
Wouldn't need either of 'em by themselves, I s'pose.*

Ponder that.

*Let's see, what else can we throw into the mix? Grav-
ity . . . that was a nice touch. How many kinds of gravity
do you think there are? I mean, there could be a spiritual
gravity. Thoughts certainly seem to gravitate. As do friendships. Hmm, friendships . . . complicated, that. Oh! . . . and
of course there would be us . . . lot goin' on there, too; intricate stuff like awareness. I'll bet that which created shared
awareness on every conceivable level—interactive awareness—no doubt on levels we couldn't begin to imagine.
Throw in a healthy dose of reality, then stir. Huh . . . if it
weren't for the reality part, what would awareness have to
be aware of? What game plan is underway, and how exten-
sive must it be?*

He moved freely within his feelings, bathing in the
thought and the implications lying therein. After a
time, he took the feelings with him, found his bearings, and began moving back to the present. It was

a slow, arduous process. There were mountains to climb and memories to traverse. He remembered the earth in flux, all the little skirmishes, the jostling for position; life had been raw and not terribly orderly. Then came the first drop.

Irony trickled into every fault line. Looking back, that first raindrop had been a strange and foreign experience, a bizarre happening destined to fade into oblivion, a quirk of madness, nothing more. Then there *were* more, and life had become slowly, inexorably, civilized. And, for the first time, he got the connection: raindrops not only melted mountains, changed scenery, and altered the course of events, but they were the catalyst bestowing civilization on a desperate world. No wonder Barkmoore treated Reanne with such reverence.

As the mystery of it all swirled around him, he tried to pull the pieces together, hoping to understand how a tree and a raindrop fit into this picture. But there was no way to fathom the depths of their secret worlds. He wondered once more how Barkmoore gained such knowledge and why Reanne had remained silent. Just what was she up to?

These and many other things ravaged the gullies of Iggy's mind as he quietly rose from the depths.

Chapter Seven

Reanne moved slowly, feeling with small tentacles the nature of the life form that kept her from rolling off the rock's edge. At first she thought moss to be a benign creature, but soon discovered deeper intentions. It was engaged in a relentless digging that removed bits of material and, small as they might be, erosion was taking place. Iggy didn't seem to mind, though. Perhaps he enjoyed the company, or maybe he liked the coolness that was provided. Either way, he was off somewhere, and an answer lay out of reach.

"So what *does* 'mind is the realm of promise' mean?" she asked no one in particular.

Iggy had been able to catch the last bit of her question, surmising its entirety. "You want to take that one, Barks?"

"No, Ig. Please, go right ahead."

"Well, all right. Reanne, I, ah . . . hmm. Maybe I should rephrase that. Mr. Barkmoore, would you be so kind as to take that one?"

"Mr. Ignatius, it would be my pleasure. You asked me what I saw, my radiant little friend, and in deference to your life-sustaining proclivity—for which we are all profoundly grateful—I will do my best to do my best to . . . "

The furrows on Iggy's brow eased, and a smile creased his face. Barkmoore smiled in the rock's direction, acknowledging his release from mild embarrassment. Although it had been the tree's intention to imitate the rock's peculiar speech, he had no idea the effect it would have on the raindrop, for she fell into full uninhibited laughter.

They watched Reanne for a while, then looked at each other, slowly coming to understand the wonderful silliness of the moment. It wasn't long until they joined her with a few quiet chuckles, then came the belly laugh, and all was lost. By the time they crawled back to the fringes of sensibility, everyone had forgotten who was saying what. Eventually Iggy said through a snuffle, "Ball's in your court, Barks. Ah, *Mr.* Barks."

"Oh, of course. Quite right, quite right."

It is difficult to describe the way in which a tree speaks. Strains of reverence and wisdom deepened by an air of certainty mingle within a fuzzy cacophony, producing the effect of a multitude of voices speaking in unison. The gentle cadence belies an underlying force of will, as pitch moves easily within a soothing rhythm, sifting quietly from a broad expanse.

"The promise of mind. Not an easy thing. It seems your hope lies within some form of understanding I may never fully satisfy, but let's have a go. Promise. Promise is rather elusive because it exists largely as a potential, don't you see. Mind, on the other hand, when used in the appropriate manner, is a unifying force, and curiously, though mind springs from a material source, it has the unique capacity to escape the material.

"So let's throw pattern—that persistent repetition of similarity—into the mix, for without the framework of pattern, without its unifying and cohesive properties, all would be lost. Pattern by its very nature is a constant and enjoys the lofty distinction of pervading both the material and spiritual worlds. It is the loom upon which mind weaves. And, oh, what a weave! For mind is not only the cradle of ideas and the wellspring of imagination but is also the gateway to the realm of spirit. Whether pattern is of a material or spiritual nature it has no choice but to interact within set guidelines, while mind is devoid of such encumbrance and may explore limitless possibilities.

"Now, let's stretch out a little. When the capacity to contemplate infinity enters the arena of mind, some level of spirit receptivity has been achieved. And you well know spiritual and physical energies are as opposite as opposites get, but what do you think happens when we, the physical, yearn to discover the source of our spiritual endowment?" Barkmoore turned toward the rock, hoping to see some of his former brilliance.

"Ah, well you'd have . . . Reanne?"

"Yes, indeed, there would be . . . what?"

The tree rustled impressively, his resonance blending with the enchanting echoes of the forest. "On some level there is communication with that very source, and if spiritual growth occurs, progress is made toward completing a circle—a level of insight. When that circle has been mastered, the next level lies in wait, and if mind so chooses, the journey continues.

As long as there is curiosity, hopefulness, trust, and a growing desire, the heights that may be attained are limitless, for spirit is always a willing partner, and therein lies promise."

The raindrop was dumbfounded. What she had seen in her vision, that which she believed to be impossible before the rock had helped alter her concept, was now cast in a new and fascinating light. Barkmoore, realizing he'd missed something, turned her way.

Reanne began in a small voice, "Before I met Mr. Ignatius here, life had taken on a sameness, and for the most part I'd lost the magic. Then the vision came, and even though I had no idea what to make of it, the future seemed a little brighter. But what you're saying adds a whole new dimension to what I saw. It's just that . . . oh dear." With a curious mixture of defiance and awe, she finally said, "How is it possible the universe has that kind of depth . . . is . . . is that organized?"

Barkmoore thought for a moment. "How is it possible? I do not know. Nonetheless, any organized structure has, at its core, purpose, and purpose plays a pivotal role in the fabric of reality. I assume we all agree the universe is a reality, and that there is organization within that reality.

"At first, I didn't see it very well myself; then by juggling a parameter or two, I began to notice how things commonplace were really quite striking, once you thought about them in a different light. Drudgery may be easily found, but once one begins to master the art of rising above the din, one discovers an astonishing creativity framing the very things and places that once seemed so ordinary. And to what purpose? Now there's a question." He moved in a way that drew Reanne's full attention.

"Your and your friends' every journey may seem commonplace, but those journeys have an unquestioned value. Well, in your case, perhaps not so much."

"How would you know about that?"

"Just a guess."

"Oh."

"They may be meaningless exercises in futility to you, but to us . . . "

"I never said they were meaningless. I simply meant sometimes there's not much to distinguish them from . . . "

"From what? The one before?"

"And before that."

"I suppose. Reanne, promise is only that—promise. One has to act on the premise that journeys are a part of some greater purpose lying within the intricate weave of reality. A weave fashioned within pattern, given impetus by spirit, and made unique by personality and intellect.

"It may be difficult to see the purpose of your journeys at first, but think of it this way. How could Original Mind make us an integral part of an ever-progressing universe if we knew from the beginning how everything worked and what the future would hold? It seems our Creator wants us to learn firsthand, for the process of discovery brings value to meanings and meaning to values, and your journeys, my friend, are an essential part of that process.

"Iggy stumbled upon a significant part of the mystery when he discerned the relationship between opposites. What were his words? 'The tension between the two is the glue that binds'? How could God fulfill His creative potential without the opposite of perfection? It seems the infinite requires that which is finite to pursue the Divine Adventure.

"That we err along the way is of little consequence. For it isn't so much what we do as what we strive to do that engenders growth and fullness of purpose. Without progress, without a world filled with possibility and promise, what would we inhabit other than a bereft, static, pretty much useless universe?"

Everyone stepped back for a moment, giving the thought some room. After a while Barkmoore, not sure where to go next, or if he should go anywhere, thought about Reanne's exasperation as she'd said, "How can the universe be that organized?" Implied within was "How can that possibly be, even though clearly it is?" Her quandary was something he was not unfamiliar with, and with age he'd managed to iron out some of the wrinkles.

"Fellow travelers, and I wouldn't think to use the term lightly, while you may not know, most probably will never know, how the world is organized in such away, at least now you know why. And much to our good fortune, buried in the uncertainties of life there are clues, traces left by the execution of a plan." He looked Iggy's way, a twinkle in his eye. "As you so eloquently put it, my hardscrabble companion, there are always impressions left by the footprints of perfection."

Seeing that he had piqued their interest, he thought this might be a good time. "Would you mind if I told a story?"

"Here we go." Reanne couldn't help herself.

"It's a short story, but, perhaps I've already said too much. If you'd prefer . . . "

"Oh, no. Please go on . . . just a reflex. I'm . . . oh dear." Reanne flinched.

"No need for worry. I find your manner . . . oh, let's see . . . somewhere near the curious side of refreshing. Not sure why, but I do. Just thought you would enjoy a tree's perspective. Perhaps this will shed some light on, not so much how life is organized, but the manifestations lying therein."

The tree's branches rustled softly as he began: "No current moves far without intermingling, without facing the consequences of past deeds, and no one escapes the current. Life's current begins at the center of the universe—any sapling will tell you that. It's a rather specialized viewpoint. In the beginning, all we know is what we feel inside. Everything is new and nothing is certain, save the notion that all begins here and we are safe in the bosom of creation. There is a sublime understanding, a certainty that life will never end. It is a wonderful time to experience the sheer unbridled joy of being alive; it also foreshadows, to every new and helpless member of creation, what endless possibilities the future holds. Then one day we find ourselves immersed in the current, buffeted by other currents as they, too, search for meanings and direction.

"Adolescence is accompanied by a curious mixture of idealism and dissatisfaction, with no short supply of rough edges. It is often a dangerous time for those of us, how should I put this, that have a more complex structure than your esteemed but elementary designs. I hope that I didn't . . . "

Iggy shrugged. "No offense taken. We know what we're made of."

Barkmoore returned a warm and thoughtful smile. "As the ragged edges of youth give way to the polish of maturity, entirely new concepts emerge. Some are transitory, others take root and grow. Then there are those that can't be proven either way. With such a welter of could be's and should be's, it is sometimes difficult to know which path to take. Early on, though, out of simple curiosity, I chose the path of inquiry— the unraveling of mystery. And through all my years no mystery has caused more bedevilment, or dismay, than the one of which I am about to speak.

"As a society, we tend to rely on the concepts and notions of those who have gone before. For some, homage paid to the legends of yore is a required rite of passage one does not question; customs and traditions lie sacrosanct, no thought given to the distortions of time. Now, I've no doubt a good many of our traditions are based on truly astonishing events—but to be set in stone?"

Iggy raised an eyebrow.

"Folklore and rituals are curious in that we, as a collective, are predisposed to believe them unassailable, and while some of them are fascinating, and some of them even ring true, there are those that just don't sit right. Seems to me a little objectivity is in order from time to time, though I hear the words 'sacrilege' and 'blasphemy' bandied about at the mention. Never understood why, and it pains me no end, no one pays attention, nor is thought given, to the signs lying quietly in the brush: telltale clues to the many and varied ways our Creator reveals Himself to us, one of which I would like to share with you, if I may take the liberty."

Nodding approval, they settled in.

"By the time I had learned to stretch the boundaries of my imagination, discerning what was possible and what was not, my children were in various stages of asking the question 'why.' And one day, while watching them wrestle with concepts beyond their years, it came to me just how subtle is the voice of God. I remember shadows dancing playfully, Mr. Ignatius, on your worn and wonderfully unassuming promontory, and while I was tracing one particular shadow for no apparent reason, several thoughts converged, creating an impression."

He paused for a moment of veneration.

"It came to me how utterly impossible it is to become a parent without first seeing the world through a child's eyes. I ask you, could there be any more wonderful system, one more replete, more absolute, than to have the advantage of watching our children grow from the viewpoint of that very same experience. As parents, we can understand love, mercy, and forgiveness from a Creator's point of view because we have already experienced and know intimately the trials, travails, and incompleteness of a child's world. But it gets even better, for it is also an opportunity to glimpse the inner workings of spirit in some personal way, to know intimately the love, mercy, and forgiveness with which God looks upon us. It is undoubtedly one of the ways God communicates with us.

"I knew it was a message. I don't mean a message that was thrust upon the scene. I mean one that was lying in wait for someone who was searching. Life is littered with signposts, all waiting to come into phase with . . . "

Watching his friends' faces, Barkmoore lapsed into silence.

Clearly they were baffled; curious, but at a loss. Apparently he had misjudged the vastness that lay between their worlds. He'd known from the onset there would be complications and that meanings might get lost in the mix, but surely they would come to see the implications buried within a simple observation.

Guess not.

Chapter Eight

Neither the rock nor the raindrop could fathom the tree's desire to impart such intimate knowledge, nor did they understand the significance of the tree's words. Iggy came the closest. He knew that the universe revealed itself individually to everyone, and he'd seen his own version of the signs. They were scattered everywhere, like debris after a storm. He also understood that conversations with the infinite always took place in slow motion, and that time had an intriguing habit of exposing what was once invisible, and a way of bringing to light that which was worthy and real. But this thing about children; some chasms weren't meant to be crossed. He felt a sudden weariness.

While Iggy took his rest, Reanne was contemplating stirrings from the past, recollections brought on by Barkmoore's foray into concepts above her station. Over the years she had watched civilizations take root and grow, only to falter and succumb to the flames of extinction. Then there were civilizations that for some reason flourished, oftentimes evolving in the most surprising of ways. She had never really understood the underlying cause, or what pressures had come to bear, but there was something of the process's inner workings reflected in the tree's words. She wondered if the rock had noticed the connection and looked his way, soon coming to doubt the likelihood.

"Ig, what are you doing?"

"Huh?" He yawned.

"You weren't sleeping in class were you?" The siren's smile reappeared.

"No . . . no, I was . . . just . . . " Before completely shaking off his semi-slumber he spoke out of the mist. "I had children once."

Reanne giggled. "When did you ever have children?"

"Oh, a long time ago in a collision. Pieces flew everywhere. My long-lost sons, buried in a rockslide," he said, pretending to be crushed.

"I guess I deserved that. Do you practice being silly or does it come naturally?"

"Comes naturally."

Reanne grinned, oblivious to the moment.

Barkmoore rubbed his branches with a touch of resignation. "Suppose I should've seen that coming. Hoped for better, but there you have it . . . is what it is."

His disappointment didn't stem from their irreverent behavior so much as an undercurrent running through the forest. No one seemed happy with his decision to speak as freely as he had, and for the life of him he couldn't see why. Perhaps they were afraid some natural order was in the process of disruption, leading ultimately to the demise of their God-given dominance over the realm. He'd never been able to dismiss the twinge of sadness that accompanied his years of disappointment—as a group they were far from enlightened; religious devotion was not the same as spiritual discovery.

Long uncomfortable with this notion that they were the chosen ones, he had done his best to instill a different way of thinking, only to be rebuffed by a congregation clinging in near desperation to ancient beliefs of an angry god filled with retribution. As the perceived loss of divine favor overwhelmed their desire for truth, the fear of change ran through them like fire.

Having no desire to live his life in the stagnation of ignorance, he had chosen to break ranks with the forest, ignoring the shrouded comments and blatant stares. Now he once more ignored their protests and smiled upon the rock and the raindrop.

Of all the fascinating things he had seen, and there had been many, none could compare with the events that were unfolding before him. He saw a complex network of bridges connecting three very dissimilar components of creation. There was an overlapping of corners, a unity of thought, and a common desire for truth. Something in the mixture opened a door, and he saw for the first time the forest for what it was—a work in progress.

Pattern moves freely within levels, connecting one to the other, he thought. *Why didn't the rest of the forest find that to be a fascinating occurrence? Iggy saw it. He's studied levels within levels, and the similarities inherent within them, from the micro to the macro.*

Civilizations were like that, he thought. There were striking similarities inherent throughout their structures.

Interactions moved within the very same patterns—top to bottom—whether it be siblings, the family, or the clan, right on up through the higher groupings of society, nation, and global community. On scales large and small, there was progress as configurations of interaction and awareness evolved—the inheritance of a divine technique of creation.

This forest, though, ignored the signs freely given, refusing to move from one level to the next. On the odd occasion, he would detect a breakthrough to a higher level of thought on an individual basis, or at most, some enlightened discussion within a cluster of trees, but always they were suffocated by the overwhelming disapproval of society.

He could see that almost every tree in this forest, on this level, found comfort in the certainty that there was sufficient information to remain complacent, to feel secure in the status quo. One day though, through the grist of evolution, as concepts matured, they would see a different picture, one slightly altered, one more pliant. There would come a day when all would agree that there was no place for self-righteous certainty, they would come to see that their most precious endowment was the capacity to explore possibilities. And, though those possibilities would lie within the limitations of any given plateau of comprehension, the process itself would raise levels of awareness, shining a light on the next level.

One day they would come to understand that the Lord walks by their side, urging them forward as they traverse the territory, a territory framed within one overriding constant: He smiles upon us equally, whether we be grass or tree, rock or raindrop. He smiles upon us as we do our own children. And not one among us would deliver an iniquitous child into eternal torment. How could they believe the Eternal Father of Mercy could entertain such thoughts? But they did. One day, though, concepts would clarify, and they would reach out to that distant level, and it would welcome them.

This revelation brought his attention back to Reanne. It came to him that she was searching for the overall picture, something that must be terribly difficult to find when always on the move. He began speaking to her in a way that also spoke directly to his brethren:

"My wonderfully radiant friend, surely after all this time, you must know that as children of the material world we have limitations, but access to spirit is not one of them. Your confusion should be no reason for concern. The material world, ever in its state of flux, creates some rather interesting vortices, and no shortage of demons—some genuine, others imagined, and sometimes it is difficult to disentangle the two. There is a dark side: luring ghosts of ease and power, delusions of grandeur, hatreds that become all consuming, fanaticism and the like.

"Even so, vortices abound for a reason. Though they may blow strong with the winds of imperfection, they are meant not to harm but to stimulate, to kindle the fires of personal progress. The eddies swirling around us have little to do with the inevitable blunders of shortsightedness. Meanings well said sometimes find themselves lost in the ripples; hopes and dreams become tangled in webs spun with other goals in mind, and good intentions can find the going treacherous, becoming caught in currents no one could have foreseen." Leaves on the lower branches ruffled slightly. "Even so, all is not lost. Confusion may be inevitable in a world awash with diversity, but as Iggy will tell you, there is always a light within to guide you along your way."

Barkmoore paused for a moment, considering the prospect of extricating himself from what had been a surprisingly enjoyable and refreshing encounter. There wasn't much more he could say, really, and surely they had plenty to think about for a while—well, more than a while. When the irony dawned on him, he couldn't help but smile, whispering to himself, "S'pose time's something they won't find in short supply, eh?"

Peering over an endless array of canopies housing diversity beyond imagination, he took in the enormity of it all. The forest completely dominated the realm and yet somehow it seemed so small. Feeling eyes pressing upon him, he turned to Reanne, who seemed to glow. Barkmoore would have loved to discover the source of her satisfaction, but knowing any attempt would be futile, he simply said, "My friends, do not be troubled that the potential for evil exists. In what other way could goodness reach the sublime heights of mercy? A perfect world with no mountains to climb—where would the impetus for greatness lie? From where would the satisfaction of conquering our personal demons come? That we are compelled to make decisions is perhaps the most remarkable of all the gifts we take with us as we traverse the uneven paths of an ever-changing universe."

A single leaf floated gracefully to the ground as the tree embraced the rock and the raindrop with an affectionate smile. "Maybe we should add one more concept to that which defies definition: If mind carries us into the realm of promise, and time gives us the ability to redress, then must hope be the child of spirit. We are here to find out why. All we know is that harmony is our hope, fellowship our desire, and divine service our destination. Choose your paths well, my friends. The journey has only begun."

As the wind found other pastures to breeze, the tree bowed one last time and spoke no more. Somewhere, perfect mind looked out over the universe, finding within the vastness of space one particular jewel of creation. Infinite joy nodded in acknowledgment as one rock, one raindrop, and an assortment of trees worked their way up the spiral staircase.

Part Two

Chapter Nine

Iggy and Reanne reached longingly for simpler complications, for the quiet reflections of the river, each with a different imperative etched indelibly upon their respective structures, each hoping secretly to cross the impossible bridge between them.

So we have wings, and we can weave, the rock thought. *What possibilities lay there? What new adventures lie ahead thanks to . . . trees are cool.*

Reanne nudged him gently and said with the siren's smile, "Yes they are."

"How do you do that? Nobody else does that, how do *you* do that?"

"It's a gift."

The twinkle would have worked its magic on almost anyone else, but Iggy was becoming used to her ways, was beginning to move within the flow of a raindrop's world. Perhaps this was the time to nudge *her* a little, to find out if what he suspected was so.

"At what point did you begin to realize you were almost in over your head?"

Reanne's twinkle remained true, but a momentary distortion in her shimmer told a different story. "I think I'm still in the process of trying to figure that out." She stared at him, her smile slowly fading.

Iggy had an impish grin. "I suppose you're wondering how I knew that? Well, I can assure you it's nothing terribly mysterious. *I pay attention.*"

"To what?" Her stare had not wavered.

"The little things."

"The little things? Pray tell why?"

"Because, they're the ones that make all the big things."

"Oh."

"But that doesn't mean it's easy, I'll tell ya that. Thing is, when you first dropped onto my doorstep, I had just finished a series of contemplations, none of them really going anywhere. Hadn't found anything even resembling a piece of the puzzle in ever so long . . . this puzzle of existence . . . the way things work and all. I've known for a long time an underlying force was at work here, and that it's hard to see, but the lack of progress was driving me to the short end of hope. Who would have thought such a thing would fall so neatly into place? How often does the world turn on its lamp . . . shine on new horizons?"

With an interesting mix of disquiet and release, Reanne's expression moved within her words. "I'm still a little wavery on the last part, but the short end of hope sounds familiar. Another three or four hundred thousand cycles, and, whew, I don't know what would have come of me. One loses sight of the goal to the point that the big picture is a blur, and there seems little reason for going on. I have to say, when you came up with that bit about the ordinary becoming extraordinary simply by changing one's perspective, I honestly thought you were delusional. Now I see you just shine different."

Iggy couldn't think of anything to say.

They shared each other's company in silence, closing the gap that moments ago seemed so formidable. And that seemed good enough. And realization came to the rock—a raindrop is happiest when on the move, using her natural ability to the fullest.

"So, Your Radiance, should we call it a day?"

Although his invitation to leave gracefully was very much appreciated, at this moment, it was the last thing she wanted to do. Some small part of her continued to register alarm that this dull, unassuming but amiable stretch of hardened earth could so casually rip her open, exposing her innermost self.

"I don't know. I'm confused about a couple of things. I don't understand what events would transpire that could lead to this end. I really don't see it. Rhyme and reason aside, when all is said and done, things just happen the way they happen. But sweet Patricia, this had a texture to it.

"I remember the clouds and falling free, and I remember the overpowering joy a moment like that brings. But in the midst something crept in, an odd sensation gently pressing me, nothing I couldn't ignore if I wanted to, and I wanted to. God, I love free-fall. Nothing down here compares to it. No stream, no raging torrent, no wondrous confluence or waterfall, just that one moment when life holds its own and . . . oh dear, what was I saying?"

"You were falling free."

"Oh yes, yes. So I was. Well, I was falling, and the earth kept getting closer, when I had this premonition. I didn't know what to make of it, so I just pushed it away. It's curious now that I think of it; the ground may have been coming toward me, but when I set that feeling aside, my joy returned and you were gone. Well I'm sure you were still there, but at that moment . . .

"It's funny how in those kinds of situations reality seems so far away, like it doesn't even exist. And then the weight returns. It always returns, doesn't it? Like some ghost out of . . . I don't know what. After awhile I didn't have much choice. The ground was nearly upon me, and I didn't see how I could miss it, so I was hoping for a nice soft landing somewhere in the trees when this gust came, and . . . did you know that you look like a grayish-brown speck from way up there?"

"Really?"

"Yeah, you were kind of handsome actually, in an ominous sort of way."

"Ominous? Wait a second . . . are you saying that I'm . . . ?"

"Oh, come on, Ig! If you had the choice of falling free for a long, exquisite, wonderfully delicious ride with a nice cushy landing, or crashing into a big hard object, which one would you choose?"

Iggy had to think about that.

"You are impossible. I'll tell you this: I was in no particular hurry to find out what you were like, and I certainly had no intention of talking to you. I just really hate brutally hard, messy landings, and venting steam always seems to help."

"That bad, huh? In case you haven't noticed, messy tends to be a reality thing."

One eye half closed, she said, "Yeah, uh huh. You have no idea what we go through, Mr. Reality. And to top it off, as I recall you were a little . . . shall we say, derisitorial?"

"Sorry about that. It came to me you might need help adjusting to reality."

"Nice try, Ig."

"Hey, always go for the open door."

Reanne laughed, giving in. "Well, now that I know rocks think about things beyond their own prescribed little worlds, I'm beginning to wonder if that feeling had something to do with you." She looked at him closely, "Naw, that couldn't be. All I know is, once I landed the feeling went away, then things unfolded in a way . . . sweet rolling rivers of grace, you don't think the wind . . . that gust that sent me past the trees . . . ?"

Iggy rubbed his chin in an efficient sort of way. "Wait a second. Are you saying that when you landed there wasn't a game plan, no agenda whatsoever . . . that you never talked to a rock before?"

"I try not to. Ok, yeah, I knew something was up, and I had some ideas, but things turned in directions I never saw coming."

"What does that mean?"

"It means, even if there was some force orchestrating all this, I would think it would have better things to do than concern itself with our insignificant little worlds, but apparently there's more to it than that."

Silence ensued as thoughts curved over the divide, their faces painted in shades of uncertainty. After a while, Reanne felt the unmistakable beginnings of Iggy's rumble:

"Do you think this mysterious force you're almost referring to rolled the dice just to see what would happen? I mean, there must have been a game plan somewhere."

Reanne shook her head. "I don't know if it works that way. I'm telling you, stuff like this just happens. At least, I think I still think that."

Iggy stared into space and imagined for a moment how simple complexities must appear to the intelligence he had seen moving in lines so adroit, smooth and powerful. New appreciation crept through his crystalline circuitry; electrons followed one another, desperately seeking alignment, forming a picture.

"I can't say for sure that I know for sure, but, remember what I said about chaos being the raw material? Well, there you go. How can something be built without raw materials? We're the raw materials, and a complicated stage has been set, giving us something to work toward. There is potential in varying degrees in everyone, and no one in particular is singled out, but eventually, by sheer force of numbers, someone breaks through and progress occurs, hopefully passing the information on. I mean, what just happened here was a breakthrough of some proportion. We all understand each other a little better, and where that will lead there's no telling. Follow me for a minute here.

"If the whole is made of individual parts, all imperfect and all searching for center, and working toward a common goal without common definition as to what or where center is, that would set up a rather interesting ballet, wouldn't it? The whole is a thing of beauty even if the individual parts and their interactions may at times be less than charming.

"Imagine the dance. Some gliding over the floor alone, some with partners, others in groups of varying size, moving at various speeds and directions, each with an agenda, everyone interacting in ways that may or may not have any meaningful structure. But, from a larger point of view, it's a work of art—the structure of the whole stays in balance as it moves forward.

"I mean, look at the way gravity works. There's a constant but not unyielding force that keeps things from falling hopelessly away. With us, there's the same kind of cohesive force working behind the scenes. All of our hopes and dreams, aspirations, and yearnings will in one way or another find fulfillment or disillusionment, success or failure somewhere along the line, but whether they go one way or the other doesn't matter. The point is, is that there are positive and negative forces working within a dynamic, moving everything forward in a controlled and orderly way, creating a never-ending dance that stays within set boundaries.

"It's as if chaos is part of the process of infinity working toward perfection, trying different combinations, constantly creating new situations—tilling the earth, if you will. Of course, if that were to ever happen, if the universe ever reached absolute perfection, the whole thing would cease to exist, because the tension between opposites would be gone . . . what am I saying, that can't be right. Something would happen, though. Probably something cool." He looked her way for confirmation. "So, what do you think?"

"I think you haven't the slightest idea what you're talking about."

"Yeah, but it sounded good."

"I'll give you that." Reanne turned toward the horizon and watched the last storm remnants disappear. In their place, benign formations came to life, growing swiftly with the heat of day, their changing configurations challenging the sun as it searched leisurely for weakness. There was a give and take, a playfulness that seemed natural, and there was majesty. As she watched, the meaning of Iggy's words began to unfurl.

"So, balance can be a delicate thing, not unlike the difference between what is believed and what is actually true, what is known and what is not, even how something is perceived. If truth is an absolute, the confusion stems from the infinite number of variables in any given . . . " Her face went blank for a second. "I really don't believe this. Now I'm starting to sound like you."

Iggy chuckled, eyes gleaming, as Reanne swerved from exasperation to a semblance of lucidity. "Balance . . . hmm, life begins, then spends time working out inconsistencies, hoping to find . . . " She whirled to meet his stare. "Ig, do you find it odd that trees come and go so easily, hoping to find . . . what? What *are* they hoping to find?"

Iggy's moment in the sun turned on its head. Reanne hadn't so much turned the tables as brought a new one into the room. And it was a curious table, indeed. Iggy didn't know exactly why he should find such behavior odd, but he did. And he found it even more curious that Barkmoore had never addressed the question of his survival directly. What did happen to civilized forms of life when they passed through the portal? Perhaps reference had been made, but never in a way that came anywhere near being succinct.

Having no desire to respond with an answer that bordered on speculation, he surveyed the landscape of his uncertainty. There were no clear markings on any of the maps, no guidelines for a situation that could easily stray from center, that could offer no more than leanings as truth. What could he say about a tree's mysterious appearance and disappearance? It was something quite beyond his imagination, this coming and going and learning and knowing. And what did Barkmoore mean when he said consciousness was either there or it wasn't? Did that mean that if it wasn't there it was somewhere else, or did he mean that it wasn't anywhere at all? Depending on the circumstance, it might go either way. Why hadn't he mentioned that, and where would Barkmoore's consciousness go once his branches lay bleaching in the sun? No matter how hard Iggy tried, it always came back the same. Speculation would have to do.

"I find it odd because the concept escapes me. It all seems so normal, but if you think about it, it's really quite extraordinary. I mean, how can someone as smart and powerful as Barkmoore grace this planet for such a short time, then cheerfully leave here without so much as a goodbye and not go somewhere that will put his hard-earned knowledge to use? I think he sees life here as a springboard. To what, or perhaps better said to where, would be a good question."

"To where? You really think there's a where?"

"Yeah . . . yeah I do . . . has to be. Been studying them a long time . . . seems they think of this place as a spawning ground."

"A spawning ground? You can't be serious. Where do you come up with this stuff?"

Iggy hesitated. "Have you ever heard of the Gathering?"

Reanne froze.

"I think you're right, it *is* time for me to go."

He could feel her moving purposefully, feel the delicate pull of moss as her grip began to loosen. This was not good. Once more his voice was low and commanding.

"What do you know?"

She continued making preparations for departure, unwilling to look into his eyes. Iggy remained silent, which was the last thing she expected. Almost out of the moss, curiosity got the better of her. "So, you want to know what I know. First, you tell me what you think you know of them, then we'll see."

"They aren't always here."

It took some time for her to realize that that was all he had to say. Finally she asked quietly, "Why do you think this is so?"

"I was hoping you would tell me."

"You want me . . . you think I'm just going to . . . oh no you don't, not this time, big fella."

"They get together when something extraordinary happens."

"Like what?"

"Like when there is an unusual shift in energy flow, or a sea change in events. They watch and take notes. I think they're emissaries."

Reanne nestled into the moss, more out of shock than for comfort. "Do you see them now?"

"No one ever sees them, but they're here."

"And you know this?"

"I believe it to be true."

"What makes you so sure?"

"I wasn't until you . . . until now."

"You son of a pressure pot, you gypsum-garnet wannabe!"

"That was cold."

Reanne was in a delicate situation. She didn't really know all that much, and she wasn't sure who actually did. She had only talked of the Gathering with other raindrops. They were a topic of particular interest, mostly because not even a raindrop could see them. Sometimes though, things would happen, little things no one could put a finger on, small differences that might be no more than coincidence. While the patterns were elusive, they were enough to engender discussion, and someone like Iggy had never been a part of those conversations.

"Sorry, didn't mean to hurt your feelings."

"Say no more. What's a few harsh words between friends?"

Both of them searched for center, Iggy finding equilibrium first. "I've felt their presence before, but I don't think anyone else around here has. I was wondering why, and I was wondering if they sent you."

"Oh, my goodness, no."

Her lighthearted response settled one of his questions, but he felt the undercurrent. There was no point in going in that direction, though. Raindrops did like their secrets. Even so, her intransigence made his attempt to tie the Gathering to Barkmoore's eventual departure difficult. He tried again.

"I find Barkmoore curious because there is something magical about the way he and his lot exist. I often wonder about them. How exactly did they get here? All of the things that go into the making of a tree: me, you, the wind, and I'd be willing to bet the sun . . . there is nothing in us that would lead one to suspect something like trees could happen, but there they are. And even if I could get past that part, could understand the math, I doubt I'd ever be able to figure out how they begin, how they become. They just do. It is completely beffafeling.

"I didn't really get the meaning when he was talking about children, but little bits of what he was saying are beginning to seep in. From what I can piece together, they start out fresh and new, completely untainted. They see the world for the first time with no preconditions, no agenda, only awareness. Then he and his kind blossom into these well-meaning, problem-solving creatures that go way, and I mean way, beyond anything that could possibly be the culmination of the elements and energies they're made of, only to give it up, to be replaced by somebody that comes out of nowhere."

He stopped for a moment, wondering which way to turn, when a new picture formed. "Have you ever seen a line of fire work its way across a field? Interesting sight. It appears to be one large singular entity, but if you play the tape slowly in your mind, what you see are blades of grass giving it up one at a time, each releasing an individual flame as it's consumed.

"Looking at a forest, all you see is a forest, right? In reality it is a succession of trees who live and die.

No one notices a forest change when one tree gives it up anymore than they see a change in the fire line because one blade of grass is gone. But here's the trick. Instead of moving across a field, a forest is like a fire line moving through time. Somewhere down the road we'll be here and so will this forest, but everybody in it will be new, will be different. Kind of spooky, isn't it? I tell you, Reanne, something, or someone, somewhere is doing some pretty interesting stuff."

"My, Iggy, you do go on."

"Yes I do."

Reanne had never really thought of it in that way. To her, what was, was, and there had never been any reason to get into the details as long as her missions had been completed more or less successfully. Now perspectives were changing, making her wonder if it wasn't time to rework a few notions of reality.

Looking deep into the forest, thoughts of her vision intermingled within the images stretching before her. A quiet movement bore relentlessly from every camp, probing for possibility, pressing toward propriety, toward balance. Dark greens and browns danced within the reflections of what few sisters remained as they toiled cheerfully toward some common goal.

Her eyes dwelled within the recesses, eventually moving out of the darkness into clearings shadowed by bark-clad behemoths, beings who stood in silence, formidable in their solitary pursuit. Her thoughts moved within the shifting tide of possibility as her vision brought into focus a forest canopy impossibly intertwined. It seemed no amount of effort could untangle the interplay, the relationships of harmony and interdependence.

A growing brightness streamed through variations of sorrel and emerald, drawing her attention to open sky. The sun moved carefully, unobtrusively. In time, shafts of light came to life, shining majestically against the clouds. Her focus danced in time to the rhythm as pillars of silver, gold, pewter, and rose slowly splintered, forming canyons, their walls nimbly adjusting bearing, hue, and range. It was a spectacular display. She watched for a long time, inspiration slowly seeping in . . . *If a rock could think of all this stuff, what more could a raindrop do?*

What could indeed!

"You have a say, Barks? The Gathering ever cross your doorstep?" She knew there would be no response, but deep in her heart she knew he knew . . . something. *Hmm. If one had a notion, how would one go about . . . ah, yes well, may perhaps.*

She studied Barkmoore's countenance, her thoughts escaping where they would as leaves rustled gracefully, and she could have sworn he winked. Well, *okeydokey*, she thought, then with a rippling and eyes turned to flint, she said in a language known only to trees, "Thanks for the nudge. So much for meaningless exercises in futility . . . shall we dance?"

Chapter Ten

Reanne was careful not to make contact with the other raindrops as they fled Iggy's surface in ever-decreasing numbers. She was virtually alone now, which was the only way this could work. She refocused on the vision that seemed a distant memory, recreating in her mind the lines of force and their exquisite interplay. Some of the lines ran true while others played off an interesting set of points.

"So *that's* what that was."

As she worked her way into a secure position within one particularly towering ridge of moss, Iggy watched the transformation take place. He thought he'd seen almost everything. Now he looked on as the raindrop moved into various positions of a convex nature, as if searching. He would have interrupted, but this was all too curious. Time went by, soothing wonderful time; thought-inducing, sleep-oriented, sun-going-down kind of time.

When the raindrop's focus came within range, lines of energy began to appear that once had been invisible. Their significance remained unclear, though, for she had no point of reference nor personal experience from which to make judgment. She watched in fascination as the vision moved before her. And having no idea what any of it meant, she was adjusting her focal point, hoping for some form of clarity, when there came into view a door from behind which a familiar light shone.

And there, what she would have thought beyond the realm of all possibility, lay a field of stars. And she saw that each one was of a different hue, precisely as they had been in her first encounter. And once more there walked through the stars a shimmering visage, and as before, the apparition touched the brightest one and smiled upon her. This smile, though, no longer held an uncertain air.

Buoyed in such a manner, her bewilderment surrendered to the wiles of temptation. Embracing the moment, she was drawn into a world beyond the scope of words as lines of force streamed around her in a cascade of contours and color. After a bit of time, patterns began to emerge, providing points of reference from which to make judgment. And in time, relationships uncovered themselves, and there formed before her eyes a picture astonishing in its symmetry and unequaled in its beauty. And, though, every aspect flawless, the relevance to her notion of reality escaped her.

So it was her foray had ended in, if not abject, certainly undeniable flames of failure. Downcast, she was in somewhat of a quandary, when the image began to flicker. Then, in a flash, it grew to a stunning brilliance as the presence moved near, and she could feel there was something more it wanted her to see. Closing her eyes, a simple revelation came to pass, and the light vanished.

Measured, sonorous vibrations danced in and out of range. Her senses disoriented, she looked around blindly, trying to remember where she was. The vibrations gradually turned into words, emanating from a voice dimly recognizable. As her sight returned, light bathing her in a muted opulence, her expression turned to surprise.

"Um. Ah . . . what are you doing here?"

"Well you see, a long time ago there was this cataclysmic change in events. A great tremor deep in the . . ."

"Oh, quit," she said, poise just around the corner.

"Nice to have you back."

Silence ensued as Reanne assessed what had happened and slowly put the pieces together:

"Have you ever . . . oh dear, do you think it's possible to see things that are . . ."

Iggy felt a warm glow. His search for meanings had always been a lonely endeavor. Now someone shared his passion, and together they trundled along, bound by the quest. It was more than he could have ever hoped. Embracing the moment, he said with the requisite sophistication and decorum, "Well, yeaayah . . . that's what I've been trying to . . ."

Iggy's voice there but not, she looked out of the moss toward the heavens. "The Gathering is only . . . the deepest reaches of thought can't begin to . . ."

"Where *did* you go?"

"Those lines you saw, the lines of power, did they move in threes?"

Iggy thought back and studied the flow of force. There were lines of power stretching into oblivion. He could see they were indeed loosely grouped in threes, but the surrounding activity was such a jumble of confusion. There were intertwining configurations, fluctuating shadows, and patterns. There were just so many.

"None of this makes sense."

"Look again."

He looked deeper, altering internal perspectives; deleting, filtering, processing:

"Well, I'll be a pebble's pappy."

"Yeah, that's what I saw, too."

Iggy watched as his notion of the world turned upside down. The fact of existence and the origins of life had always been shrouded in mystery, but no one ever doubted the material world was the fount. Now it seemed that wasn't entirely true.

What he had seen in each grouping were three main lines of power flowing within the fluctuating shadows, the significance of which was uncertain. Of the three, one was obviously material, another clearly the most powerful, but of unknown origin, although there was no doubt it was spiritual in nature. The third line, however, while moving in tandem with the first two, shifted periodically between them as if in communication. This line was particularly curious, for it held no resonance that signified alliance with anything other than self-determination.

What at first he had taken for fluctuating shadows moving freely between the three major lines of force, he was now beginning to see, were the laws of physics moving in a relationship not unlike tides chasing the moon. What had confused him was the intermingling of two distinctly different activities. There were the triads, and there were the fluctuating shadows, which appeared to be of little consequence, but were in reality their own very powerful force.

This revelation sent his mind back to the beginning, to the dominant line in each triad. If it was spiritual in nature and the dominant line, what did that say? He studied the shadows once more, and their peculiar movement.

Well I'll be.

The shadows weren't fluctuating at all. They were reflective, reflecting power from the dominant line onto the material. And then he saw something else. The third line had almost no interaction with these same reflections. But . . .

A shiver worked its way through his fissures. What *was* that?

Iggy looked around to find his bearings, aware that some of the nearer rocks were staring at him. He wasn't sure what they were thinking, but one thing was certain: they were missing out on some pretty interesting stuff.

He very much wanted, at this moment, to communicate with the unseen Gathering of celestial beings who surely were there, to ask them questions and to have them confirm what he thought, or thought he thought. There was something he didn't quite get. He wondered if they had in some way reached out to him, or had that never been part of the plan. Had they instead let him work things out on his own? He suspected the latter. In his mind he could see them: glorious inhabitants of a world beyond his wildest imaginings. They moved with grace and dignity, emissaries from a level of existence that undoubtedly had its own limitations. *Levels within levels*, he thought. The world was so very mysterious.

Reanne was staring at him, too.

"Iggy, I'm wondering . . . are we seeing this the same?" Reanne wasn't exactly quivering, but her shimmer had never radiated as it did now. "Seems up to this point our conclusions have been somewhat limited. I think I'm beginning to see what Barkmoore was trying to tell us: that physical laws are a reflection of the patterns of spirit. I'm not sure exactly what you saw, but with all that was going on between the lines of force, I came to one very simple conclusion. There is a different and astonishingly powerful world pervading the world we consider to be real: one very active and far more enduring, one that . . . "

She paused, resting her thoughts on the world's fulcrum.

Iggy saw that picture, too, impressed with her interpretation, knowing good and well he'd never finish that sentence either . . . there was, however, a *spark*. Rummaging through memories, hoping to find something that might have escaped his attention, something he would have passed over because it carried no relevance at the time, there came into view an old friend. A concept that had often been little more than hazy notions or vague images slowly came into focus in the most delightful way. He began pulling up, and sorting through, pictures, occurrences, and impressions of the way things always, at times inexplicably, seemed to work to the good. As he did so, there came upon his countenance a smile.

Reanne, bewildered, but hopeful and determined, muttered, "Barks mentioned something about the laws of dynamics as, how did he put it . . . elaborate sentries?"

"Extravagant sentries."

"Extravagant sentries to the world of order. What exactly *is* the world of order?"

When the last piece fell neatly into place, he said, "I'm not sure, but I think it has something to do with circles. I just ran a comparison chart, and it seems circles tend to absorb and direct energy flows. A bunch of little engines is what they are. I think if it wasn't for them, energy would just go off willy-nilly with no hope of ever reining in the chaos that runs rampant in this world. No matter which way you turn, or what may transpire within any given body of work, there is always a circle involved. Some you'd hardly know were there unless you paid attention."

She moved a little deeper into the moss, mumbling to herself, "Point taken."

"Reanne, what qualities do circles possess that would account for them being such a subtle but dominant force within the natural world? And what does that have to do with the world of spirit? How would you even begin to make sense of anything like that?"

Iggy and Reanne wore the same expression, one of contented amazement, tinged with determination, the rock finding a ledge upon which to lean first.

"Remember, a little bit ago, we were talking about the way a circle begins and ends? Maybe there's a clue in there. What if we were to take a journey, one that ends where it began. Even though, once home, something invariably has changed, and even though time has passed, separating the beginning from the end, a circle has been completed. Then there is another journey, then another and another, each time returning to the same place. But something is different, and the differences multiply. Is it still a circle?"

"Don't be silly, what else could it be?"

"Turned ninety degrees, the view is nothing resembling a circle."

"I'm not sure I'm following you."

"I thought we'd been here before."

"Oh, yeah, when you said life was a spiral."

"Well, in the same way a spiral can conceal itself within a circle, spirit conceals itself within the material world."

Reanne's shimmer fluctuated slightly, then came to full glory. "Oh! Oh my. So circles lie within the world of order, which is under the control of the laws of physics, which are controlled by and lie within the circuits of spiritual force."

"Appears to be so."

Once the thought had settled in, Reanne turned and asked, "Could it be that simple?"

"I thought so a minute ago, but now I'm not so sure." A smile formed that held a bit of mischief. "There is this one other thing."

"I'm not sure I want to ask."

"Yeah, well it's just that it seems we're only looking at half the picture. And this gets a little muddled because the half that I don't understand is pretty well hidden. Barks said something about mind being the gateway to spirit. So I'm wondering, if the material world is governed by the laws of physics, which in turn are controlled by the patterns of spirit, and if mind is the gateway to spirit, wouldn't there be a completely different set of laws governing that? Aren't they two completely different things?"

"Well I suppose so, but . . . "

"I mean, if the laws of physics are used in such a way as to project order onto the material arena, then what projects order onto the arena of mind?" He looked directly at Reanne.

"How do you come up with this stuff?" She tried to put all the pieces into place, and couldn't. But she had to concede it was an interesting point, and she found herself muttering into the breeze, "How would you even begin to figure something like that out?"

"I don't know," Iggy said with a touch of resignation. "I'll bet Barks knows, but I don't think there's much hope in asking him. He must have worked it out somehow, though."

"My guess is he looked for signs lying in the brush," Iggy said quietly.

"Yeah, he would, wouldn't he." She was enjoying the effects of the wind as it rippled over her surface, and as she watched the movements, a slim thread dangled in front of her agile mind. "If in the material world, an object in motion tends to stay in motion, in the spiritual world the analogous would be . . . what?"

Iggy pored over the question, completely absorbed in the moment. *Just keep it simple, you big dummy. Relax and let it flow.* It wasn't long until his eyes lit up. "I guess someone searching for spiritual realities would continue searching, would have momentum, reason to stay focused."

Reanne could feel the low vibrations as Iggy reached for meanings.

"I wonder," he said, "if that's the journey Barkmoore was talking about. He and his kind search for the embrace of spirit the way you and your kind search for the embrace of the river. You think?"

"How would I know? It seemed to me he was just as interested in whether the journey began."

"Yeah, you could be right about that. When he said that promise is a potential while mind is a unifying force, did you understand what he meant?"

"Sort of."

"I didn't. But now I think I'm beginning to. When he told us the 'parent's relationship to the child' story, there was more to it than I thought. He implied that a child is more potential than anything else. I'll bet there are implications that run deep, once set in perspective with the 'promise of mind' story. Because I think what he was saying was that for those with the potential to go elsewhere, mind not only needs to choose whether to embark upon an adventure of such magnitude, but it must also pursue, with the trust of a child, such a destiny."

She thought for a moment. "That could be. Barks seems to be at peace with the idea that trust goes a long way. Instead of spending his energy hoarding the vanities of this world, he gains strength through communication, through a real effort to harness the gentle persuasions blowing through the universe. It seems the child within him is still reaching out, but reaching out in a way tempered by experience, and based on a certainty not easily gained."

Their eyes met.

"Well, do we see it the same?"

"Appears to be so."

Reanne nestled deeply into the moss as Iggy looked past the blue, out into the heavens. And he tried to imagine what was really out there, how it all worked, and where he and Reanne fit into the scheme of things.

Chapter Eleven

Stars burn deep from within, density forcibly ejecting electrons from their homes as they spew energy in their wrath. A hard, raw, brusque, seemingly chaotic energy, all seen as mundane and orderly from a distance.

Planets move in concert, taking what energy from the sun distance will allow. They move not in a random haphazard tumult, but in a perfectly synchronized, harmonious plane, a work of art whose beauty is magnified by the enormity of their creation.

Systems move without effort, following pattern, forming galaxies that differ from one another only in nuance. These galaxies number beyond imagination, and not one varies from a simple basic plan.

All these energies visible to the naked eye hold less than one percent of the activity making up a universe. Much is taking place for reasons unknown, but what is held from view fortifies that which is seen.

And Iggy thought of these things. And while he couldn't begin to know with precision how it all worked, he came pretty darn close. And, Iggy being Iggy, he wondered what kind of activities filled the days of spirit-led beings, and he wondered about the boundless energies of a Creator and how orderly must those energies be.

He wished he could understand it all better. There were so many marvelous intersections, so many bridges that connected the arena of thought to what the eye could see, and then there was this most wonderful curiosity of creation, a raindrop. Reanne must have wishes, he wondered what her world was like and if her wishes ever came true.

"So, tell me how you did that. Not long ago you were so sure there was no 'whatever that made all of this', now you're running the fault line."

"Am I supposed to understand the reference?"

"Huh? Oh, yes . . . no, I don't know. I hoped . . . I meant see the differentials. How did you see the correlation between lines of energy so very different from each other? Some of them aren't exactly visible, or at least they don't seem terribly important, not in a way that would make sense."

"Yeah, I noticed that, too, and couldn't imagine they'd be there for no reason, so I began altering my vision, making comparisons. And here it's better I don't get into detail, but there were some interesting things going on after I went through that door—you know how they are, come out of nowhere. This much I *can* say: there were patterns, every one some variation of the major line, the dominant one we've come to know and love. But I knew there had to be more to it than that, and no matter which way I turned couldn't find anything that would complete the picture. Not even a hint. So life having a life of its own, it wasn't until I was about to give up that the most extraordinary thing happened. Suddenly, in a blinding flash, I saw what all those patterns had in common: all of them together, in their entirety, are the Creator's way of sharing everything there is to share—from the biggest to the most tiny—with all of Creation . . . which is pretty cool."

She looked at him, her eyes bright and full of life. "Help any?"

He thought for a minute. "Well, in a way, 'cause I figured out the circles part, and I figured out that the spirit world gives life to and sustains all of this here material creation, which is in a lot o' ways what you saw, but something tells me there's something I don't see that you see . . . so what am I missing?" He looked away, then turned back and said with a playful edge in his voice, "And how come you can do this stuff and nobody else can?"

Reanne had a look that said, 'I was kinda wonderin' that myself,' but went on with, "Remember when I said my eyes would become a lens? Well, it's actually more complicated than that. My whole being becomes a lens, focusing on a perspective. The problem I had so long ago was never knowing what to do once something was zeroed in, so eventually I gave up. Now there's a different stage, and . . . "

"You become a lens?"

"Yes Ig, a lens. After an experience like that, perspectives come into focus, which brought me back to what you've been saying about opposites all this time. This is where the little things, *don't wanna hear it,* come into play. It dawned on me that opposites require and are always relegated to the number two, and, as you so cleverly put it, there's a whole bunch of middle. I couldn't figure out what the middle line of the triad was, the one that moved back and forth between the material and spiritual, so I focused on the fluctuating shadows, hoping that would be of some help. After awhile it occurred to me that they were in reality something much different, something much more powerful. I watched how they intervened on the triad's behalf, how they connected with the myriad lesser forms of energy as if some sort of bridge. All of a sudden I realized what I was seeing: the laws of physics, the tensile strength of a universe. It was the reflective nature of the shadows that tipped me off. I knew that the laws of physics were extremely rigid, so I realized the way they reflected off the major line, the one that was spiritual in nature, was the mechanism that kept them from breaking continuity with the unbelievably beautiful contours of the triad. Once I figured that out, I noticed how the laws of physics hardly interacted with the third line, which I thought odd, until it dawned on me. What's the one arena in which physics has no power?"

"I'm stumped."

"Come on, Ig. Think!"

Iggy retraced his steps, following the ever-changing contours of the triads as he watched their interactions. *What had Barkmoore said? "Whether pattern is of a spiritual or material nature it has no choice but to interact within set guidelines, while mind is devoid of such encumbrance and may explore limitless possibilities." So, if the material world is the projection of the patterns of spirit, the one material thing which can transcend the physical world and comprehend the possibility of spiritual realities is . . .*

"Mind." This was barely audible.

Iggy smiled a rare and beautiful smile.

Reanne negotiated a familiar path within the moss, enjoying her newfound freedom within the world of discovery. Things were coming much more quickly to her now that she had crossed the threshold. "It's all really quite simple. The material and spiritual lines are opposites, while mind is the middle. The infinite variations of thought, reason, imagination, and emotion are held within mind. A rather extraordinary way to connect opposites, wouldn't you say?"

Iggy was still working on the revelation that the most mysterious line in the triad, the one that held no resonance which signified alliance with anything other than self-determination, was in fact mind. If reality bent to the Creator's will, and mind is self-determinant, that would explain a great deal. Specifically, the ramifications of free will. He worked Reanne's last statement into the mix and discovered he was still unclear about one thing:

"You become a lens?"

"Ig, why do you always . . . yes, a lens." She had to stop for a moment and remember he was, after all, a rock. "What I see depends on a lot of things. But I suppose that's the point, taking the effort to work through the chaff." There was a brief interlude while she thought the whole thing through, then she wondered where next to turn.

"You know, Ig, it just came to me that the number three is often more than one plus one plus one, that once the third dimension comes into being, infinity becomes a work of art." Her expression shifted within the possibilities. "Barkmoore said something about math being a universal language. I wonder, if we were to use that as a guide, what would we maybe find, speaking chaff-wise."

Iggy found that to be a reasonable idea, and he began with a preliminary comparison chart: If a two-dimensional spiral had a life of its own, it would move how? Outward. Just keep moving outward from a point, like an ever-expanding curve drawn on a flat surface. It could perhaps move in infinite ways, but it would be constrained to that one surface, while the same spiral in three dimensions could move wherever and however it pleased. Or however and wherever the demands of necessity pleased, creating enchantingly beautiful and intriguing portraits—definitely more than three.

"Reanne, what did you have in mind?"

"Well, I'm not sure, but one has to begin somewhere, wouldn't you think?" She thought for a moment, deciding it best to begin at the beginning: "A one-dimensional world would be . . . what?"

"Is this the lens thing? Ok, don't look at me like that. A one-dimensional world, that would be a point."

"Or a line."

"Or a line. But if you turn a line on end, it would be a point, which would be invisible. Come to think of it, it would be nonexistent because the line itself has no height or width."

"Yeah, it would, wouldn't it?" The raindrop hadn't thought of that. "So what would happen if you took that line and bent it until it came back to itself?"

"Ahh . . . yes. The ubiquitous, underappreciated-yet-dauntless engines of stability, industry, cohesion, invincibility, and, more often than not, invisibility . . . well said, but, as much as I love your line of thought, where are you going with this?"

"A line fulfills the requirements of infinity with the greatest degree of economy when it becomes a circle. The fact that it is still invisible when turned on edge doesn't diminish the fact."

"No, it doesn't." Time passed. "Be darned . . . what are you saying?"

"I'm not sure." She said this in a firm but curious manner.

Electrons flowed as Iggy thought back to what the tree had said about signs lying in the brush, and it came to him that conversations with the infinite may well take place in slow motion, but revelation was instantaneous—one was obvious, one not so much. So if conversations and revelations are opposite forms of communication . . . could one use that as a guide? With that thought, he began working on a new concept. A circle is confined within the boundaries of a two-dimensional world, and, at the center, which is in opposition to the actual circle, there would be a point . . . *oh, that's good!*

"Reanne, where is the center of a circle?"

She hadn't expected that. Trick questions always seemed so simple, but she knew better. Still, there was only one answer. "Smack dab in the middle."

"Yeah, but where exactly can you pick a place and say this is it and it doesn't get any smaller?"

Reanne began moving once more into various positions of a convex nature.

Iggy was fascinated but he wanted to make his point. "Think one-dimensional."

She found a position and stayed there. "Turn a line on end and it disappears." Her face was a mixture of insight and confusion. Then everything collapsed. "If the center of a circle doesn't exist . . . but it does exist!"

"So they say."

Reanne whirled. "Who said that?"

"Oh, that's Speedy. He comes by this time every day. What's goin' on, Speed?"

"Cruisin'."

"What's the word?"

"You guys are tryin' to figure stuff out that ain't exactly easy. I got some advice, and you should do good to remember this: it's always darkest before the storm."

"That's good, Speed." Iggy shook his head and turned to the raindrop, then looking back toward the snail, started to say something, but thought better of it.

"Reanne, you said a circle turned on edge disappears without damage to its significance, but does it really exist?"

"Yes . . . no . . . hmm, it seems it ought to, but I don't know how it could."

"What about shadows?" They both turned toward their newly arrived guest and stared. Speedy raised his long neck in slow motion and, looking into their astonished faces, smiled at them.

Shadows?

Reanne's confusion turned to a deeper, more profound confusion. In her befuddlement, she turned toward the perfect spiral towering above her where light splintered into shades of slate and pearl, shining with a luster that complimented the exquisite spiral that curved with an astounding, almost regal beauty.

Then she noticed that on the ground, at his foot, lay a shadow, one that encompassed an area where light refused to go, leaving a darkened impression of the snail with a curious omission—the spiral itself was gone. She moved into a slightly smaller position, increasing magnification. The implication slowly dawned on her. If that shadow left out such a splendid feature of the reality that was the snail, and we are in some way a shadow projected by the spiritual world, how blind to the realities of that world must we be? She spoke through the mist of contemplation: "If the material world is the Creator's shadow, what must the center of creation, the dominion of spirit, be like? I'm speculating here, but it ought to be pretty woofty."

"Woofty?" Iggy raised an eyebrow.

"Yeah." She seemed secure in her pronouncement.

"Think you'll find that world at the center of a circle?" Speedy arched his neck again and cocked his head to one side. "I don't think so! But there is very little that can't be found *between* the center of a circle, which can't be found, and *pi*, which can't be found."

Iggy and Reanne turned to each other and blinked. Neither one had the slightest idea what to say, though Reanne was still in wonder of the moment and disinclined to say much of anything anyway.

Finally the rock asked, "What does pi have to do with anything?"

Speedy lowered one antenna. "What have you two been doing all day? You sure haven't been paying attention, for Pete's sake! You've been making enough ruckus to wake up the whole valley, and what have you got to show for it?"

Iggy looked at Reanne and whispered, "Do you think Pete knows Patricia?"

The snail shook his head. "Is he serious?"

Reanne suppressed a chuckle, but the smile was there. "I'm afraid so."

"Well, in that case, I'm beginning to see your predicament. Let me see if I can help. Ig, you do know what a radius is?" An affirmative nod was enough. "It's a line. A simple line . . . actually a line segment, but we'll call it a line. Curious lines they are, too. They're in infinite supply, invisible, and unerringly *uniform.* No one gives them any thought, though. Sad thing that, because the relationship between the radius and circumference produces a number, pi, that is also infinite, invisible, but unerringly *random.* Don't you find that curious?

"An elusive number created by countless invisible but uniform lines, coming from a center that falls into infinitesimal eternity. It's as if someone is saying you can have everything in the middle, but the inner and outer limits are mine. Puts a swagger into your theory about opposites, doesn't it?"

Iggy stared at the snail with a sense of disbelief. "So let me see if I understand what you're saying. A circle has a center, whose existence is in doubt, an endless array of lines emanating from said center, whose existence are in doubt, and a circumference whose very relationship with said lines is defined by a number whose end is in doubt."

"Kind of a metaphor for life, isn't it?" Speedy had never actually stopped moving. He had a tendency to slow down when engaged in conversation, but the world was a big place, and time was running short.

Regaining his momentum, he searched from side to side, deciding on a path that would take him to a lush patch of grass growing at the bottom of one of Iggy's steeper ledges. "Expand that onto a three-dimensional stage and things start to get interesting."

"You mean a sphere?" Reanne's eyes lit up.

Speedy, more interested in the grass, didn't answer right away, giving Reanne time for reflection. She began to ponder the significance of the third dimension. She thought about the way life, nature, and pattern tended to reflect the triune underpinnings of the highest levels of universal cohesion, even of God Himself. Surely the snail saw that and might even have a better grasp of the way things really worked, for he seemed to understand the concept in a way she didn't quite.

"So is the circumference the result of the lines or does it create the lines?"

The snail came to a halt and lowered his antennae until they pointed straight toward her. "How do you describe something complicated without using complicated words?"

Reanne shrugged.

"You use simple words."

"What are you saying, Speed?"

"They all work together—the three parts of a circle—each having their own part to play. The same is true of dimensions. A sphere can't exist in two dimensions, and it will tell you a story if you take the time to listen. It's one of the signs Barkmoore was referring to—the third number is that pervasive, and that powerful. Only one of its kind, it is.

"If you use it as a guide, you may find that there are three kinds of work: physical, mental, and spiritual.

You may find there are three states of matter, and three primary colors. You may even spend your day deliberating on the abstrusions of past, present, and future. But three dimensions means that the Creator bestows upon us the gift of possibility. And possibility is a big place."

Chapter Twelve

It was a mystery to them how Speedy moved with such grace and apparent ease. Hidden in his movement were tiny undulations. Had they known this, much would have been revealed, they would have seen in miniature the pulse of a universe.

As it was, Reanne absorbed the various concepts, oblivious to the revelation passing before her, soon finding a flaw in his phrasing. "Possibility is a big *place?*"

Speedy just nodded.

Guy seems sure of himself, I'll give him that. She knew possibilities were endless, but still, a place was somewhere that you were, or going to be. *Unless you thought it was where you* might . . . *huh. Ok, I get it. One never knows for sure . . . which breeds a whole world of curiosity, and no end to aspiration and desire . . . can't forget imagination . . . and just to liven things up, throw in the odd miscommunication . . . then there's good-old-fashioned hope and the search for a better way, and on it goes. Go that direction, and . . . clever little urchin.*

While Reanne had to work the inference through, Iggy had no illusions. He had no doubt Speedy was referring to something other than an actual place. He'd been on many a journey without going anywhere, and there were plenty more places to go. What clouded his world was this pesky little knot he couldn't untangle.

"Speed, if we have the gift of possibility when the third dimension comes into play, what happens with two? I mean, there's all kinds of possibilities with opposites, don't you think? Or, well . . . I'm not sure I'm sure about this, but maybe it's like the spiral where there's a pretty big difference when you add the third dimension. Actually, a really big difference, but still, does that relegate two to irrelevance? Or just to a sorta kinda thing that hopes for the best?"

"Haven't heard such eloquence since, since can't remember." That bit of sarcasm tickled Reanne no end. Speedy gave her the slightest of nods, then rising to full height, slowly shook his head, blinked twice, and peered down on the rock with one slightly crooked antennae, "You *are* a dense one aren't you? All this time you've studied opposites and never got the connection, huh? Ever heard of prime numbers?"

"Well, yeah. There's a bunch of 'em in stuff I was working on this morning. Found this progression that has a shine to it. Came to me years ago watching leaves blow around in the wind, in one of those little tornadoes. See them enough times, you notice they're darn particular about the way they behave, and the whole thing gets bigger, the same way those numbers do. Only lasts for a little while though, 'cause often as not, the ragamuffins aren't far behind, and all the leaves go back to ground." Thinking maybe he shouldn't have said it quite that way, now that they were friends, he turned to Reanne. "Uh, no offense, I, I didn't mean . . . "

She shrugged, "None taken, you big galoot."

"It's just that sometimes when you come around, you come in droves and change everything. Have to say, though, that sound you make is pretty nice, makes up for the leaf thing. I tell ya, Speed, there's nothing like it." He looked in Reanne's direction, seeing a tinge of skepticism there. "No, really, I mean it . . . puts us right to sleep."

She did her best to resist, but temptations are what they are. "Ig, you are truly gifted. As long as I've been around, I've never seen anybody dig a hole that deep without moving. And the thing is, you do it so effortlessly. I am impressed."

"Yeah, well . . . it *is* soothing. I mean, how can you not enjoy that sound, and you guys keep the dust and grime off. That's important. And helpful . . . and . . . "

Speedy looked at him with dismay, shaking his head. "Ok, now that we've established your capacity for genius, let's get back to the point. Primes have a number of interesting correlations, but we were talking about opposites . . . the forlorn two."

"Oh, right. Well, I did notice that the stuff I was working on had a lot of prime numbers in there, like I said, but I haven't the foggiest what that means, except for the windy part, and can't for the life of me see the connection with opposites, or the number two." A strange look came over him and he looked at Reanne. "You guys don't have anything to do with that, do you?"

"What?"

"The fog."

Reanne and Speedy shared a moment, letting the big galoot work it out. Finally the snail said, "Prime numbers, there's a whole bunch of 'em. And every one is an odd number. Every one. An infinite parade of numbers, all odd, and you can't come up with something about that that's a little *odd?*"

"No, not really. What's so odd about that?"

"Use your imagination, Ig. Think of a big place, of the possibilities."

So the rock did. He ran through picture after picture, going back in time, then reversing course. He took special note of anything that overlapped, or bent a corner, anything that stood out. He did find one little bump on the horizon, and slowly it began to dawn on him: "The voice on high can be subtle, can't it?"

Speedy smiled with delight, even came close to a slow little jig.

Iggy, though, was stunned. How could he have missed something that had been right there all this time? *"Two.* The number two is an *even* number. And it's the only one. Out of all those numbers. It's . . . "

"That's right, my friend. There's no way to get to three without going through two. Show me something so powerful and profound, something as pervasive and consequential as the duality in nature."

"Yeah, I'll work on that."

Speedy laughed. "The opposites you're so fond of, and so fascinated with, for darn good reason I might add, are a unique and essential component in the fabric of reality, which is something I guess you already know, but prime numbers, in their own way, will tell you that, even if you didn't. It's a stretch of the imagination, I know. There, nonetheless.

"But here's the thing. As big of a lunkhead as you are, you're this close to discovering the third pillar of nature's noble triumvirate. The numbers in the progression you were foolin' around with this mornin'—one plus two is three, two plus three is five, and on you go—are every bit as important as pi and prime numbers."

Speedy looked at Iggy quizzically. "You really have no idea what you're onto, do you? You know, you really area big galoot."

When Iggy responded with a blank stare, the snail came to a full stop, and turning around, began moving toward Reanne. "Seeing as how you seem to be the brains in this outfit, and seeing as how you were admiring my shell a little bit ago, which, as lughead here would say, you didn't think I noticed you noticed, what do you think? Where lies said implication?"

"You're going to have to help me out here. I really have no idea what you're talking about."

Speedy looked to Iggy and said, "You ever notice how secretive the little ragamuffins are? No idea what I'm talking about. Been all around the world, and has no idea what I'm talking about."

"You really wanna go there?" Reanne said in her best stern tone.

"Yeah, I do." Speedy said right back.

She knew the ins and outs of the concept, being a founding member. Her configuration was, indeed, the very beginning of the progression—one, two, three—one oxygen plus two hydrogen. It was a simple thing. Take two highly combustible gasses, combine them, and form the most perfect, versatile, life-sustaining creation in creation—water.

Even she marveled that the progression found its way into every corner of the material world. Then when life graced the planet, and proliferated, it did so in an astonishing array of form, size, and splendor, all using in varying degrees the same progression. The fact that all of life was imbued with the "magic proportion" could only speak to the divine plan, which was naturally beyond comprehension.

She and her friends had carried on lengthy debates as to what it all meant. The only decision they'd ever come to was that they should keep this to themselves until there was a consensus, or there was some compelling reason to do otherwise. Since that had never happened, she had to hedge a little.

"You know, I've wondered about that. What is it that makes the way you grow so fascinating? And yes, can't help but admire your shell. It's one of the many things in my travels that is always a delight. I never get tired of the effect, and always leave realizing I've just seen something special."

He looked at Iggy. "Damn, she's good."

Iggy just nodded.

"Ok, I see what I'm up against here. You two are in cahoots, and I'm gonna tell ya anyway 'cause you're both just so darn adorable, ragamuffins and lugheads that you are. My great-great-grandpappy and his grandpappy and his goin' back over three hundred million years, mind you, *are* a part of somethin' special. When the good Lord put all this into play, he didn't fool around. The guy's pretty smart and he came up with a plan that made everything grow and move in such a way that they weren't butt-ugly and there was a modicum of grace attached to it. So those numbers you were tryin' to figure out this mornin', Ig, are the mechanism that makes stuff work really well. And they're everywhere and in everything, dang near. Now Reanne, was that so goll darn hard to tell me, even though you coulda? What is it with you knuckleheads? Part of creation and always these secrets. I'm gonna let you off the hook, though, 'cause I know you got your reasons. Just wish one day you'd clue me in. Not askin', just wishin'." With that, he turned and made his way once more toward the grass. Smiling as he went.

Silence embraced the land.

And time passed.

And Iggy thought about that.

So it was he found himself on the eve of shadows, moving within the current, a current that apparently had no end and spent its day enjoying the fact. The current of time. *There is but one current that carries every idea, notion, thing, or purpose within a universal rhythm*, he thought. *Even something as timeless as spirit moves within time's boundaries, providing the pattern that that rhythm moves within.*

And time is beholden to no one.

And he wondered about that.

As he did so, an odd thought came his way. "Speed, if three dimensions are the provision within which infinity finds the means to foster meaning and possibility, and if a line fulfills the requirements of infinity with the greatest degree of economy when it becomes a circle, and if a sphere—a three-dimensional circle—is balance personified, why isn't pi an even three? Why does it have that little bit extra?"

"Beats the heck outta me. Maybe 'cause a circle isn't three-dimensional. Maybe that odd little bit is what kicks it into a spiral."

"Well, I'll be darned. Quite right, quite right." He thought for a minute. "No. No, that's probably not right."

"Yeah, I never believed it either. But I keep hopin' to find a connection."

"You're a different breed, Speed."

"I'll take that as a compliment. You're not too bad, yourself." With that, he made his way to the edge and ambled out of sight.

"All right, let's see what we can make of this. There's one time, two opposites, three dimensions, and the possibility of something that ties them all together. The simplicity of complications," he sighed.

Reanne sighed, too, working on her own complications. Between what the rock had said—that opposites were held within limits by some pervasive force working for the *good of everyone*, and what Speedy had said about the opposites inherent within a circle being *off limits to everyone*—the logical conclusion would be that the two realities had different origins, knowing well they did not. This gave her pause. It seemed when the Creator engaged in the realm of opposites, it registered on a different scale, quite possibly a scale bordering the far side of absolute. She knew there would be no way to fathom that. But there grew within her a light, and she began to comprehend the simple beauty held within the hidden unwavering power of a circle, any circle, no matter how big or how small, no matter what purpose it may serve, and her sudden appreciation for the precision with which randomness worked put a smile on her face.

The rock turned her way as a voice came sailing over the precipice: "Every silver lining has a cloud."

"I love that guy," Iggy said as he studied Reanne's demeanor. He could feel that in some way she had just come full circle. The light inside, which had begun to flicker, now shone brightly. He threw a soft pitch, curious. "I wonder how many kinds of circles there are."

"You mean including shadows?"

"Huh? Oh, I suppose so. Shadows don't have to be circles though. Hardly ever are."

"Yeah, but they're both two dimensional."

"What exactly does that mean?"

"Haven't the foggiest."

"Yeah, me either."

Searching into the vastness hidden by an illusion of blue, bits and pieces came together. He saw that it wasn't so much the way levels of reality tended to overlap, or that they fit snugly one within the other; rather it was the overwhelming unity of disparate structures of power that tied everything together in a way that made progress possible. And while he had no way of knowing that pattern moved so precisely that seashells, hurricanes, and spiral galaxies shared the same mathematical progression as his friend the snail, he was beginning to see that pattern rode the winds of time, creating shadows that didn't so much exist as they confirmed that which did.

Iggy wondered what the graph would look like if a line were drawn through the focal points of all the parallels life had to offer, all the patterns that wove such an astonishing and marvelous tapestry. Would it be neat and tidy, or some incomprehensible work that imagination was powerless to see? He even wondered if it would be not so very different from the spiral that moments ago moved before him.

Variations within life took intriguing paths, he thought, *some laced with quirks and not a few missteps, but there lay, at the heart, a unity of theme. The tree moved while remaining stationary. The snail's structure remained stationary even as he moved in a fluid and languid way. They were the same but different. Different only in manner, not intent. What knowledge had they tried to impart from respective points of view, and what was held in common?*

"Reanne, I've been thinking."

"Say it isn't so."

Iggy smiled his goofy smile, "It's just that there seems to be a curious intertwangle of perspectives here. Barkmoore and Speedy said some of the same things in different ways. But neither of them came right out and said what I think they were saying. What they said, they said, but there are implications that go beyond the enigmatic world of a shadow and the simplicity of a circle."

"Huh. I suppose I was kinda wanderin' down that path myself, 'cause what we saw in the vision; the intricate dance within and around the lines of force, and the way it was there and sometimes there not so much, it was as if . . . "

"Yeah, I think pretty much it was what we didn't see, too . . . like the spiral hidden in a circle." Iggy's brow furrowed, moving in time, dancing with the rhythm of his words. "Sooo . . . if we are a shadow that is cast, then must we be . . . what? In some way a part of a circle too big to see? That would explain a lot. And this much I think I think. Whoever created that circle left behind clues that point to an interesting thread winding its way through darn near everything, and my guess is it unifies diverse aspects of reality in ways no way we could ever find out. It seems the three parts of a circle projected onto a three-dimensional stage in some way reflects the triune nature of God himself, of pure spirit, and that's there for all to see."

He lay quietly for a moment as electrons rearranged themselves. Then came the light, and he began to speak with a mix of quiet authority and newborn understanding.

"What's the last thing Barks said? He said, 'Choose your paths well, my friends. The journey has only begun.' We begin in the shadows of reality, and through mind's alliance with the will of the Creator, with the reality that is spirit, we slowly emerge in some small part as real co-creators of an unfolding universe. We come to *be*, and go forth to find adventure at every turn, learning as we go, on the way traversing a landscape where confusion reigns and order ultimately rules triumphant."

He wasn't sure she would follow. Then he saw a twinkle in her eye and felt the warm glow of a vision and a moment shared.

"An interesting plan, isn't it?" she said, closing her eyes, imagining the totality of it all.

An infinite and triune being found expression, creating a circle. On its outer fringes children were made, made out of dust, given free will and a notion of spirit. Who among those children would look the Creator's way, set their path, and desire above all else to make the journey back to the center, to the Father's hearth? What marvelous works would these children create together along the way?

As the majesty unfolded before her, the sun nudged clouds aside and set the river on fire.

Chapter Thirteen

Iggy had seen the fire many times. It reminded him of a resurrection, a moment in which the world held magic and hope for a better day, though his deepest chambers couldn't begin to hope for what would come next. Moisture conspired with the setting sun to envelop the forest in an iridescent glow. Ruby-laced emerald dominated the realm while traces of sapphire sparkled in the distance, complementing an otherworldly display that shone against the darker moorings of wood, earth, and rock. Light seemed to come from everywhere and nowhere, dancing within the ever-changing play of shadow.

Mesmerized by the spectacle, he barely caught the rustling of branches somewhere within this ghostly milieu. Shifting his gaze, he beheld a vision of majestic proportion. High in Barkmoore's loft, there a falcon perched staring into the distance, surveying the land with fierce penetrating eyes. Leaning forward ever so slightly, she ruffled her feathers and flexed her talons, then all was quiet, expectation hanging in the air.

Iggy watched in anticipation as wings unfurled, effortlessly taking flight. The transition to freedom was striking in its scope, and alien to a rock's world. The agile form rose in long powerful spirals, soaring ever higher until it found a thermal, then hung motionless, eyes intent. In a blink, as if finding a precipice from which to fall, the great bird folded its wings and disappeared from sight.

Iggy blinked, took a breath, and let out a long, rambling, "Wooow."

All was quiet for what seemed a very long time.

Slowly Iggy made up his mind. Time for a journey. He felt tentatively for the precipice, preparing to fall with the bird into the unknown, when a thought pierced his consciousness—why *was* she here?

Moving back from the ledge, wavelets of nostalgia trickled through every fissure as his mind drifted past the raindrop to the river. Through the waning fire he saw ripples take on the same patterns the deserts had taken when shaped by the winds long ago. It had been an age when wind and sand held mastery over the realm, moving within the flow of time, creating a dance of grace and beauty overwhelming to the senses, all the while leaving him with a vague impression of loneliness.

Now all had changed.

This dance with the raindrop was much more powerful, and was complicated in ways that challenged his imagination. It moved within the framework of ancient times, but brought to light something new and irresistibly different.

Which was pretty cool, and made him wonder, "So, what was the deal with the tree? You two had something going on I didn't quite catch."

Reanne's face turned in surprise, slowly changing to a thoughtful stare.

"Oh, just planting a seed . . . can't really tell you about what, it's a raindrop thing. Meaningless exercises in futility and all that. 'Sides, couldn't let Barks fight the good fight all alone, could I? Hopefully others will come along and help out from time to time . . . no tellin' what might happen. Barkmoore certainly took something to heart, don't you think?"

"Oh, yeah. Whatever you did stirred something deep. I thought I felt activity when he first opened up, but whoa, you should feel it now. Messages are flying everywhere."

She sat back with a satisfied smile, her glow a satin shimmer.

Reanne followed Iggy's eyes toward the tree. They knew in some ways his knowledge was beyond them, but there were also levels only a rock and a raindrop could inhabit, levels a tree would never understand. What an intriguing division of labor.

They settled in, taking in what had been an unprecedented succession of moments, enjoying to the fullest time as it passed, and in the midst Reanne whispered, "It really is quite enchanting."

"What?"

"The way you do that."

"Huh?"

"Humming. You're humming . . . again."

"What? Oh. Really?"

"Yeah."

"Huh."

"'Huh,' my sweet waterfall. You got something on your mind. Spill it."

"Yeah, well . . . ok, um. Well, um . . . I was

wondering . . . I was just wondering if you could show me how you do it."

She stared at him, clueless. Finally she had to say, "You wanna help me out here?"

"The lens thing . . . how do you do that? Become a lens?" As he fell somewhere near clarity, the sun nudged ever closer to the horizon, bringing to bear the rarest of moments. A growing iridescence radiating throughout the forest began to illuminate the hidden patchwork of gem that surfaced along his side, creating a multifaceted light show of vivid reds and blues sprinkled within variations of silver and gold.

Had she seen this, she might have paused. As it was, she went forth in her genial way, "Ah . . . well, ya big lug . . . I don't think I can show you something you already know how to do. But I can tell you what I've come to know that you already know. Vision is about letting yourself go and allowing the spirit within guide you. The tree knows this. So does Speedy. He's just a little more . . . I don't know, what would you call it?"

"Um, I'd have to think about that. So you really think I can do the lens thing on my own?"

She had to stare at him again. "It's what you've been doing all day, ya dorf." She took a moment to stare at him a little more closely. "And this he apparently knows, too. You really *are* a loggerhead. Dang!

"What's he doing now, anyway?"

"Well, I do believe he's cornered a grasshopper, trying to make conversation. Got him backed between a twig and a leaf, asking him something about the evolution of species."

"You're kidding, right? What'd the leggy one have to say?"

"Don't know. Just felt him jump and land somewhere out of my range, so your guess is as good as mine. Hold on a minute . . . yep, Speed's on the move again, goin' after a cricket."

"So you're not kidding. Huh. Wonder what the cricket will have to say. Always thought they were more civilized anyway, and had a way about 'em."

"Uh, yeah, well . . . to a point. They are kinda cute, though. Never thought unkindly of 'em, 'specially at night when they . . . " Iggy's voice rose a notch, "Hey, I got it—*free spirit*."

"What?"

"Speedy, that's what he is. A self-contained, moving exposé on the merits of being a free spirit."

"Yeah, he is that. Wonder if he ever talks to trees. Interesting foray into cross-pollination of ideas that would be. Speaking of which, have you noticed how the world has changed lately? Lot more viewpoints, and some of 'em are pretty dang good. Kinda makes you wonder what's down the road, doesn't it? Whaddaya think Barks would say about that? Not that you'd finagle him into any such.

"Gotta tell ya though, much as I love all God's creatures, just always had a special affinity for trees. And now that I've met Barks, I can see why you're so high on 'em. He's way ahead of his time, just like you said, and God bless the pioneers, nutin' gets done without 'em. Dang it. Now I'm startin' to talk like the curved one. Do that sometimes. After awhile I'll get back to normal, just hope I hope I don't start talkin' like . . . ooohh daang!"

Iggy smiled to himself, thinking the turn grand.

Time stood still as they carried their separate thoughts. Reanne reached into her pocket, thinking how fickle the wind. Had this been mere chance, a random playfulness of the cosmos, or was there a gentle hand at work, a nudge reflecting some deeper intent, perhaps someone with a profound sense of irony? The last thing she'd wanted to happen was the thing she'd needed most.

Dang!

How fickle the wind . . . indeed.

And she wondered about that. And she wondered about reflections . . . and intentions. They may be different, but they were everywhere. And that, they shared. And then, too, they came to life in so many different ways, not unlike the wind.

So it was, her many and varied reflections brought forth a wistfulness, a side Iggy thought he would never see, wouldn't have guessed was there.

"Mr. Ignatius, my dear sir. This is stuff I never would have thought about before we met. Reminds me of the old days when the world was new, and there was excitement in the air. Before the endless cycles brought me down and I . . ." She suppressed a shiver. Then came the radiant smile. "There's a whole new world out there, thanks to you and your improbable friends." Coming to full shimmer, she ran her eyes over distant terrain, imagining the possibilities time held in its evanescent grasp.

Seeing the look on her face, Iggy decided it was best not to say anything. But he thought about the way things unfold, revealing an ever-expanding panoply, seamless and alive with primordial vigor. There was a progression, there was unity, even if at times loosely connected. There was timelessness, and there was now, always now.

He thought about consciousness's alliance with intelligence and the portals that opened when one found the right key. It was all very clever; no voices ever said, "Tuesday, let's do lunch," but food was always on the table for those who sought the wholesome nourishment of that which stood opposite the material, that which made the material worthwhile.

A breeze brought with it change, a small turning of awareness, and a cooling. Reanne held onto her satisfied smile as Iggy thought about the fact that she had actually called him sir. Had she really done that? Had they managed against all odds to cross the divide?

Seemed so.

Dang!

Ought to say somethin' . . . not sure what though . . . how 'bout do what you always do, go with the flow, find out for sure . . . ya think? Yeah, why not?

"Hey Reanne, don't go tellin' this to all your raggedy ol' friends, okay? No need this gettin' around . . . not sure I should even say this . . . but, well, there was a time, way back when, back about the time you were goin' through your fits of conniption with the world and all, I would have given anything to be in the flow of the river, experience the magic. I think now I know what that would be like. I . . . you are . . . "

Words escaped him, he had no intention of letting her see him become sentimental.

Reanne wasn't fooled, though, the lens was working just fine. "Well, I must say this has been an experience I won't soon forget, Your Gruffness. And

I'll not be tellin' my raggedy ol' friends, least not most of 'em," she said, laughing and kissing him on the cheek.

Iggy wasn't sure what to make of that, and was somewhat flummoxed. Well, perhaps a little more than somewhat, for he came near, but not quite to the precipice. As he wandered the hills and plateaus on his way back to wherever he'd left his senses, some-where toward the end, a bit of mischief appeared on his horizon—*maybe this would be a good time to find out something else, see just how far this could go.* "So Reanne, tell me now that you've had time to think about it"—he knew she really hadn't, but then again, maybe she had; what did he know?—"is time real or a phantom of perception?"

She shrugged, moved to the moss's fringe, and said with a bit of whimsical flair, "I don't know, Ig. Have no idea." With that, the day's events out of nowhere fell heavy, and with a preponderance of the thought, *couldn't be a better time,* there came over her a change of heart. And so it happened: a ripple formed at her core and moved outward, moved de-liberately through the fluid lattice of her structure as it searched for the surface. Once there, she whispered so only Iggy could hear, "Nature's way of keeping everything from happening at once—oh, by the way, and this just came to me, don't ask me how, haven't a clue—God made us this way 'cause He didn't want to know how it would end. Well, not end . . . unfold. Don't think there's an end."

Then she winked.

Iggy, now beyond flummoxed, looked at her in utter surprise.

For a time he roamed the hills and plateaus yet once again, his thoughts bending and swirling around and within the last few hours. He was beginning to discover that he was beginning to grasp the immense depth of a raindrop's world. *Never would have thought we were the same . . . just a little kinda bit in a different way. Huh . . . be darned.* And coming to terms with the notion, he looked out over the river, eventually whispering back, "Suppose there's little chance you'll tell me about those secrets someday."

Her response was one of unqualified, unrepressed amusement. Though, Iggy being Iggy, he knew one day she might. And having come to terms, and emboldened by her revelation, he burrowed into his cavernous vault and dusted off one of his many treasures. When he spoke, he did so with a guarded reserve saved for such moments. "There is another side to it. I've never been able to share this with anyone. You know how my companions are." He looked off in the distance, unsure. "Sometimes . . . sometimes I wonder if time isn't the constant pressure of God saying 'I am.'"

Reanne arched an eyebrow, but did not ask how he had come to sense this. Had she been able to see the iridescent display radiating along his side, it would have told her much. As it was, the sun slipped below the horizon, and the pageantry fell once more into shadow.

Within the ensuing silence, they found themselves reflecting on the extrusions of time. They thought of the bonds that were born from the mesh of opposite worlds, and the curious cross-pollination that was friendship. Before long, their eyes chanced to meet, and, seeing each other's solemn faces, they tumbled into laughter.

To Iggy's surprise, the rocks around him joined in, one by one. It seemed they had been listening after all. Iggy was slowly becoming aware that his place in the group had somehow been elevated. To what, he wasn't sure, but it felt good. Reanne bowed and twinkled, knowing how her friends would enjoy the tale, quite assured life's angles would, from this moment, be measured on a slightly different scale.

Her reflections brought various lines of power into view. They were now a part of her, and as she watched them, she noticed that they moved not unlike waves washing upon the shore. She thought of the time Iggy had spent there, watching as waves moved in infinite ways, each one the same yet each one different in some manner, and all that took place did so according to pattern, a pattern whose origins sprang from some great source, a source undoubtedly aware of what transpired here, distant nonetheless.

She could understand his passion for the entrancement. She, too, when a part of those very same waves, had become lulled into submission by the alternating exhilaration and slow withdrawal, a withdrawal that ebbed for no other reason than to prepare for the next ride to shore. A shoreline where earth, wind, and water intermingled, a place where one felt the power of unity. The rock and the raindrop had been there under different circumstances, and for different reasons, but something of the experience had stayed with them, lifting them up.

Leaves fluttered in slow, complicated patterns, watching fields of grass sway in long swirling motions as shadows danced in time to the wind. A soothing whisper rose from the river's bank, filling empty spaces with a quiet hush, a pervasive sound complementing colors as they stood guard along the horizon. Conversation and laughter echoed throughout the land, reaching to the far ends of . . . well, wherever the far ends are. Iggy and Reanne enjoyed the moment, sharing a genuine affection that may well be unique in a unique world.

The Gathering moved unseen, nodding approval, each one within the assemblage thinking privately how marvelous is the Creator's plan, how unfailingly the forces of evolution produce results approaching the sublime. They would take their leave, returning to whence they came, and relate how once more a garden within creation came to bloom, finding in wait the ever-present rays of enlightenment pouring forth, falling freely upon all who sought the Creator's embrace. Filled with the moment, they bowed in prayer, then raised their voice in song.

Listening to echoes of angelic harmony, Reanne surveyed the spectacle and tapped Iggy on the shoulder. "Tell ya what. Don't know if ever I'll make it back this way, but while I'm gone, I want you to be thinkin' 'bout this: the world just ain't that dang big!"

Iggy tried to work that one out. Couldn't quite. "What are you saying?"

"I'm sayin'. . . compared to possibility."

Iggy smiled a little as he considered the implications. The day had begun slow and easy, without expectation; then she'd fallen onto his doorstep, adding light to each day hereafter. *What were the odds of that? And what were the odds that she'd ever make it back this way?*

Naw.

That would be a long shot.

Darned long.

I mean, just real darn long.

Although . . . didn't she say? "If there's a place I want go, I'll see to it that a curve is negotiated just so, then head for a certain . . . "

Well I'll be a pebble short . . . thought it was just her ramblin' at the time; now there could might be a curious little angle on what could might be.

Finding his tongue, he said:

"Huh . . . be darned."

"Yeah, new angles always surprise me too."

Iggy just stared. Speechless.

"I suppose you're still wonderin' how I do that. Well, I can assure you it's nothing terribly mysterious. The lens thing. Works every time."

Iggy shook his head, mumbling to himself, "Dangit, need to start payin' more attention. Can't believe I missed that."

Reanne watched the river move within its magic for a bit, thinking how mysterious and wonderful life really was, and how no amount of travail could diminish the fact. And watching the currents in their playfulness, there came over her a charitable notion, and this notion was a new and strange experience, much as the premonition that seemed ages ago. That both of them had happened in the rock's proximity was more than a little curious. And she wondered about that. And she came to understand that whatever magic life held, Iggy was no stranger to any of it, and that there was indeed more to this adorable, unassuming, at times enigmatic basaltic son of a bituminous boulder field than appearance would allow.

As this thought caressed her consciousness, the evening flirtations of a songbird filled the air, and when her gaze moved in the direction of such loveliness, one Mr. Barkmoore was smiling down upon her. Her eyes registered surprise for the briefest of moments, then, dancing with delight, returned a smile only the tree would understand.

It had indeed been a good dance, and words she hadn't understood at the time echoed in her head. "If mind carries us into the realm of promise, and time gives us the ability to redress, then must hope be the child of spirit."

Well spray me with sunshine . . . goofy rock was right all along—circles have beginnings and endings after all. And somewhere in there, there's bound to be the makin's of a spiral . . . life's own little special staircases no doubt.

Who'da ever thought?

Dang!

So it was she made up her mind. Turning from the tree, she gave Iggy a thoughtful stare. "You wanted to know if ever I'd tell you a secret. Well, here goes. The Gathering is here. Best I can tell, they're well-traveled and have many interests, but mostly they go where hope goes, and hope, my many-faceted friend, flows in, around, and through you like a river . . . heard 'em singin'."

The tree rustled in a gust of wind and, bowing in his graceful way, almost touched the raindrop. She winked in acknowledgment as shadows deepened (to this day no one knows what *they* were actually thinking), playing their multifarious games within her satin shimmer. She then gave one Mr. Ignatius her best stern look. "And goll dangit . . . work on the lens thing. You already know how. Just need a little more practice, ya lazy bum." With that, she smiled her siren's smile, and, brushing his cheek one last time, made her way ever so delicately through the moss to the rock's precipice.

Variations of pink and rose followed the sun over the horizon, the transition throwing an eerie glow around a rising moon. Amidst the twilight, a sprinkling of stars peered from the heavens neither confused nor concerned, though Iggy wondered about that. And he wondered, *Do we look the same from there as they from here? 'Cause there's no way in this great big universe we're all there is. One would have to be daft to think that.* And he wondered, *Why do colors follow the sun? I*

mean, they do it every time. Told the little ragamuffin that before . . . when I didn't . . . I mean before I knew . . .

Dangit!

Well, well, well . . . my oh my, ooooh my. Don't suppose I suppose can't help but think otherwise, but . . . I mean, it has been a good dance—a remarkable space in time. And Barks was right, this journey has surely only begun. And what an extraordinary journey it will might must be on the 'morrow. Not all that sure about tonight, though.

The rock thought of all these and many other things, and he thought of these things as he watched in awe one more bejeweled and splendid sunset. As he did so he smiled, for he knew there would be many other nights filled with crimson glory. And he wondered what per chance might come his way with the next breeze, the next thunder, and the next exquisite, ostentatious display of lightning. And though in all his years of witnessing such and other extraordinary wonders—and rare was the moment he couldn't quite believe his eyes—he could have sworn he just saw the tree wave goodbye as the raindrop slowly, softly, silently, slipped away.